George Edward Farrow

The Missing Prince

George Edward Farrow

The Missing Prince

ISBN/EAN: 9783337164720

Printed in Europe, USA, Canada, Australia, Japan

Cover: Foto ©Andreas Hilbeck / pixelio.de

More available books at **www.hansebooks.com**

"THE LORD HIGH ADJUDICATOR HAD OVERDONE THE MATTER."

Frontispiece.] [*See page* 110.

THE . . .
MISSING
PRINCE.

BY

G. E. FARROW

AUTHOR OF

" *The Wallypug of Why*," and
" *The King's Gardens.*"

WITH PAGE ILLUSTRATIONS
BY HARRY FURNISS

AND VIGNETTES
BY DOROTHY FURNISS

London, 1896

HUTCHINSON & CO.
34, PATERNOSTER ROW

Printed by Hazell, Watson, & Viney, Ld., London and Aylesbury.

Dedicated

TO

MY LITTLE FRIEND

RALPH CYRIL LOCKHART BRANDON.

KNOWN AS "BOY."

PREFACE.

(FOR CHILDREN WHO HAVE READ
"THE WALLYPUG OF WHY.")

M Y DEAR LITTLE FRIENDS,—

In the Preface to my last book I told you that when I closed my eyes I seemed to see hundreds of dear Children's faces turned towards me asking for a story; and now, as so many copies of that book have been sold, I am bound to believe that not hundreds, but thousands, of little friends, to whom I was this time last year a stranger, are expecting another story from my pen.

Preface.

Some of you may perhaps have seen the very kind things which so many of the papers said about " The Wallypug of Why." Now I am going to tell you a secret, even at the risk of seeming ungrateful to them. It is this. Much as I value their kind opinion, and proud and happy as I am that my book has met with their approval, I value your criticism even more highly than theirs, and I am going to ask you to do me a great favour. I have had so many letters from little friends about " The Wallypug of Why" that it has made me greedy, and, like Oliver, I want more. So will *you* please write me a letter too, your very own self, telling me just what you think of these two books, and also what kind of story you want after my next one, which is to be a School story, called " Schooldays at St. Vedast's," and which will be published almost as soon as this one is ? I did think of

writing a story about pet animals, for I am very
fond of them ; so if you can tell me anything
interesting about your dogs or cats, rabbits, or
other favourites, I may perhaps find room for the
account in my book. You can always address
letters to me in this way, and then they will be
sure to reach me wherever I am :—

> " *Mr. G. E. Farrow,*
> " *C/o Messrs. Hutchinson & Co.,*
> " *Publishers,*
> " 34, *Paternoster Row,*
> " *London, E.C.*"

Besides being a very great pleasure to me to
receive these letters from you, it will help you,
I hope, to feel that the Author of this book is
in a measure a personal friend.

You will be pleased, I am sure, to see that
Mr. Harry Furniss has again been able to give

us some of his delightful pictures, and that his clever little daughter Dorothy has helped him. I see that she has drawn, at the beginning of this Preface, some little folks with letters in their hands. I hope that they are for me, and that there are some from you amongst them.

Your affectionate Friend,

THE AUTHOR.

CONTENTS.

xiii

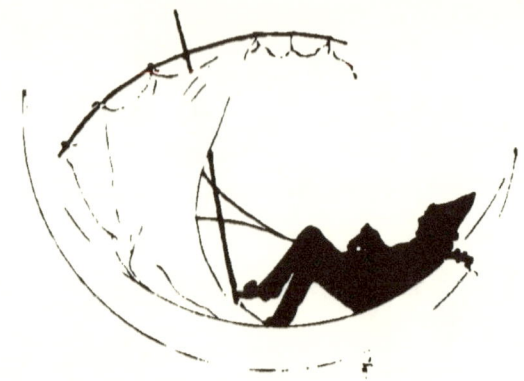

The King of Zum has passed away,
The Crown Prince can't be found, they say;
Whatever will the people do?
I'm sure I cannot tell, can you?
The way they're going on, I've heard,
Is positively most absurd,
So don't you think we'd better go
And see the fun? But really, tho',
I don't know how we're going—Stay,
I fancy I can see a way!
Of course; here's Pierrot in the Moon!
Let's go with him—he's going soon.

The Missing Prince.

CHAPTER I.

PIERROT AND THE MOON.

BOY was far too excited to go to sleep, so he lay gazing at the crescent Moon which shone through the window opposite his bed and thought of all the wonderful things which had happened on this most eventful of days. To begin quite at the beginning, he had, in his thoughts, to go right back to yesterday, when he had been sent to bed in the middle of the day, so that he might be rested for his long night journey to Scarborough with his Uncle. Then after having been asleep all the afternoon, he had been awakened in the evening just about the time when he usually went to bed, and, treat of treats, had been allowed to sit up to the table to late dinner with his Aunt and Uncle.

Soon after dinner they had started for their long drive to the Station through the brightly lighted streets which Boy had never before seen at night time, and when at last King's Cross Station was reached, they had been hurried into a carriage with rugs and pillows and were soon steaming through the suburbs of London.

Boy had found plenty of amusement in watching · the flashing lights out of the window till, as the train got further and further away from the town, the lights became fewer and fewer, and he drew the curtain and settled himself comfortably in a corner with a pillow and a rug.

His Uncle was deeply buried in his paper, and Boy did not like to disturb him, so he picked up *Punch*, which had fallen to the floor, and began to look at the pictures. He must have fallen asleep soon afterwards, for he did not remember anything else till they reached York, where they had to change trains, and where they had hot coffee and sandwiches. Then when the train started again Boy's Uncle had pointed out to him the square towers of York Minster showing clearly against the green and gold sky of early morning; and then Boy had gone to sleep again and did not wake up till they reached Scarborough, where a carriage was waiting to take them to the Hotel. Boy looked about him with great interest as they drove through the half-deserted streets, for it was still very early in the morning. He could see the ruins of an old castle at the end of the street, and as they turned a corner the sea flashing in the morning sunlight burst into view.

Boy thought that he had never before seen anything so beautiful. There was the great bay with the castle at one end and Oliver's Mount at the other, the quay and the little lighthouse, and a lot of ships, while out at sea was a whole fleet of brown sailed fishing-smacks coming in with their spoil of fish. Hundreds of sea-gulls were wheeling round and round uttering their peculiarly shrill cry, and altogether it was a most beautiful sight.

Boy's Uncle had stopped the carriage for a few moments so that they might admire it, and then they had driven to the Hotel at the top of the cliffs, and after having a refreshing wash had gone down to a large room where a number of ladies and gentlemen were having breakfast. Boy had been far too excited to eat much, particularly as his Uncle had promised him a pony ride at eleven. So as soon as breakfast was over he had stood by the window watching the people passing, till oh! joy of joys! there came to the door of the Hotel the loveliest little pony with such a long tail and mane and his Uncle's big chestnut horse Rajah, which had been sent down by train the day before.

What a delightful time it had been, to be sure, as they rode down through the Valley Park to the seashore, and what a splendid canter they had on the hard sand! And then as they rode slowly back again Boy had noticed some beautiful sand castles which the children were building on the shore, collecting pennies in boxes for the hospitals from those who stopped to admire them; lovely castles with flags and trees and toy animals out of Noah's Ark, and quaint little rustic bridges and garden seats in the gardens belonging to them, and Boy had thought how jolly it would be if one could be small enough to walk about in them. Then he had heard some one singing, and his Uncle had taken him to where a large crowd was gathered around some curiously dressed people in white costumes with big black buttons and with big frills around their necks and at their wrists; they wore black skull caps with white conical caps over these. They were called, so Boy found out, the Pierrot

Troupe, and one of them was singing about a little
Tin Soldier who was in love with a beautiful Doll with
eyes that opened and shut with a wire, but who would
not have anything to say to him because he was only
marked *one-and-nine*, while another soldier on the shelf
above him was marked *two-and-three*, till presently some
one changed the labels and marked him *two-and-three*,
and the other one *one-and-nine*. Then the little Doll
had altered her mind, and had promised to marry
him, and had forsaken the other poor fellow, who was
now marked only *one-and-nine*. Boy was very much
amused at the song, but felt very sorry for poor *one-
and-nine*, and kept talking about it all the way back
to the Hotel as they went back to luncheon, which was
of course Boy's dinner.

In the afternoon they had gone for a lovely drive in
an open carriage all through the beautiful Forge Valley,
and then after tea Boy had been taken to the Spa to
hear the band play; and now after all these wonderful
treats he was lying, as I said before, wide awake in his
little strange bed watching the Moon through the half-
open window.

What a big Moon it was, to be sure—quite the largest
Boy had ever seen, he thought, and surely, yes, surely

there is some one sitting in it playing upon a banjo! Why, it's Pierrot! and the Moon is coming nearer and nearer till Boy can hear that he is still singing about the little Tin Soldier. In a great state of excitement Boy sat up in bed.

" I wonder if he is coming here," he thought, as he watched eagerly. Yes! closer and closer came the Moon, till presently Pierrot stepped on to the window-sill and, pushing the window further open, jumped lightly on to the floor and made Boy a polite bow.

" I've brought you an invitation," he said, "to the wedding festivities in connection with the little Tin Soldier's marriage with the Dolly-girl"; and he handed Boy a large envelope with a red seal.

" Oh! *how* kind of you!" said Boy, forgetting even his surprise in the delight of receiving such a novel invitation. He hastily opened the envelope and found a card within bearing the following words:—

" Mr. and Mrs. Waxxe-Doll request the pleasure of Master Boy's company at the wedding festivities celebrating the marriage between their daughter, Miss Dolly-girl, and Captain Two-and-Three, Royal Tin Hussars.

" R.S.V.P.

"Sand Castle,
"The Shore, Scarborough."

"'I'VE BROUGHT YOU AN INVITATION,' HE SAID."

"How splendid!" said Boy. "Can you please tell me, sir, what R.S.V.P. means? I've seen it on invitation cards before?"

"I am not quite certain," replied Pierrot; "but in this case I think it must mean Ridiculous Society and Violent Papa. You see, being a toy wedding, they are obliged by toy etiquette to ask all the articles on the same shelf as the bride and bridegroom, and so the company is bound to be rather mixed, and the bride's father is afflicted with the most violent temper you have ever heard of."

"Dear me!" said Boy, "perhaps I had better not go."

"Oh, it will be all right," said Pierrot. "Whenever he feels his temper getting the better of him he very wisely shuts himself up in a room by himself till it's all over, so you need not be in the least afraid. But, I say, we had better be starting, you know; it's getting rather late."

Boy hurriedly dressed himself, and taking Pierrot's hand he stepped from the window-sill into the Moon, which was conveniently close to the window. It was very much like a boat, Boy thought, as he sat down and made himself comfortable on one of the little cushioned seats which stretched from one side of the Moon to the other. They had only floated a very little way down the street, however, when the Moon began to descend and then stopped, just at the top of the long flight of

"TAKING PIERROT'S HAND HE STEPPED FROM THE WINDOW-SILL."

steps near the Spa, which led to the seashore. Pierrot jumped out, and, after helping Boy to alight, told him that at the bottom of the steps he would find somebody waiting to conduct him to Sand Castle.

"Aren't you coming too?" asked Boy in surprise.

"No," replied Pierrot, "we must be off, the Moon and I, or people will wonder what has become of us. Good-bye!" and getting into the Moon again he was soon floating rapidly away.

Boy was somewhat alarmed at his sudden disappearance, and felt half inclined to run back to the Hotel. "Perhaps I had better go down to the bottom of the steps, though," he thought, "and see who is there;" and he had got half way down when he suddenly stopped in dismay. Why, he was growing shorter! There could be no doubt about it. He could see to his great surprise that he was only about half as tall as he had been when he started running down the steps.

Whatever should he do? Boy now felt really alarmed. Why, if he went on at that rate there would soon be nothing at all left of him.

"What's the matter, sonny?" said a tiny voice near him.

Boy looked around, but could see no one.

"What's the matter, I say?" said the voice again.

"I'm sure I don't know," said Boy, who thought that it was only polite to speak when spoken to, even although he could not see the speaker. "I am growing smaller and smaller, and I don't know whatever to do."

"Well, my little man," said the voice, "you are going to the toy party, aren't you? How do you expect to get into Sand Castle the ridiculous size that

"A SUDDEN PAIN IN HIS ARM."

you are at present? You will keep on getting smaller and smaller each step you take till you reach the bottom, when you will be the respectable height of six inches or so."

"Six inches!" exclaimed Boy. "Oh dear! oh dear!

What a tiny mite I shall be, to be sure, and I did so want to be big like Uncle!"

"Do you call six inches small?" said the voice. "Why, I am twenty times as small as that."

"Are you really? No wonder I can't see you, then," remarked Boy. "I should think it isn't very nice to be so insignificant as that, is it?"

A sudden pain in his arm made him shout "Oh!" and while he was wondering whatever could have caused it, he heard the voice repeating these words :—

"You need not think because I'm small
    That I've no reputation,
I do not hesitate to say
    I'm known throughout the nation.

"By every lady in the land
    I'm held in high esteem,
The strongest men require my aid,
    However weak I seem.

"And even you must fain admit
    That I'm both *sharp* and *bright*,
And probably will want my help
    Yourself before to-night.

"So don't attempt to 'sit' on me,
    'Twould not be wise of you.
'My name?' An ordinary Pin.
    D'ye see the point? Adieu."

"Good gracious!" exclaimed Boy; "just fancy a pin talking to one! I wonder whatever will happen next. Well, I certainly *felt* the point if I didn't see it," he continued, rubbing his arm and hurrying down the steps, for he didn't so much mind now he really knew what to expect about his size.

CHAPTER II.

THE PARTY AT SAND CASTLE.

GROWING shorter and shorter as he hurried along, Boy noticed that the Moon had gone back to its usual place in the sky, and that Pierrot was nowhere to be seen.

"I suppose he is lying down asleep on the cushions," he thought, as he let himself down from one step to another; for you see he had by this time become so small that the steps seemed like huge rocks to him.

When he at last reached the bottom one, he was greatly disappointed to find that there was nobody in sight. From behind a piece of rock, however, half buried in the sand, came the sound of laughter. "Ha, ha, ha! Hee, hee, hee! Ho, ho!" shouted somebody, and when Boy hurried up to where the sounds proceeded from a curious sight met his eyes

A Grig was pirouetting about on the tip of its tail, giggling and laughing in an insane fashion, whilst a solemn-looking Wooden Soldier was standing at "attention" and looking straight in front of him, not taking the slightest notice of the Grig or anything else.

Presently the Grig caught sight of Boy. " Hee, hee, hee ! " he snickered, " here comes a boy ! What a jolly lark ! " and he capered about more madly than before.

The Wooden Soldier, who had a label round his neck with " One-and-Nine " written on it, turned stiffly around, so that he faced Boy, and said in a deep voice,—

" I wote for you at the bottom of the step for some time, but was obligated to move to a more shelterous situation, as I am suffering from a stiff neck."

" You *wote* for me ! " exclaimed Boy, " whatever do you mean ? "

" Wote, past participle of the verb to wait. Wait, wite, wote, you know," answered the Soldier.

" Hee, hee, hee ! Isn't he a cure ? " laughed the Grig, winking at Boy, and twirling about at such a rate that it made Boy quite giddy to look at him. " He's been crossed in love, and it's touched his brain

—ha, ha, ha!—he fancies that he has invented a new system of Grammar. What a lark! Ha, ha, ha! Ho, ho!" and he rolled about in an uncontrollable fit of laughter.

"Well, of all the extraordinary individuals that I have ever met," thought Boy, "these two are certainly the most remarkable! I wonder which of them is to show me the way to Sand Castle. I had better ask." "Mr. Officer," he began, for he thought that would be a polite way of addressing the Soldier.

"His name's One-and-Nine," interrupted the Grig "What a name! Ha, ha, ha! Hee, hee!"

"The vulgarocity of this individual is unbearacious," exclaimed One-and-Nine angrily. "Let us leave him."

"Oh! I wish to be directed to Sand Castle," said Boy. "Can you please show me the way?"

"That is the purposeness of my being here," replied One-and-Nine. "Step this way, please," he said, as he walked stiffly forward.

The Grig did not seem to mind them going in the least, and kept on dancing about and shrieking with laughter.

"Good-bye, old Wooden Head!' he shouted. "You are as good as a pantomime any day, you are! Ha, ha, ha! Hee, hee!" and the sound of his laughter grew fainter and fainter as they walked quickly away from him.

"That Grig will come to a lamentuous end unless he reformationises," remarked One-and-Nine severely.

"He seems to be in very high spirits about something," said Boy.

"Yes, that's the worst of these Grigs," replied One-and-Nine, "they never seem to considerise the unenjoyability of jollyosity; they seem to think that life is all jubilaceous, whereas it is rather more otherwise than otherwise."

"Oh dear! oh dear! I do wish this man would talk in a way that I could understand," thought Boy. "Have we very far to go?" he asked at length, as they walked along in the moonlight.

"About half as far again as half," answered One-and-Nine absently. "I beg your pardon, I mean we shall be there with considerable soonness. You must excuse me being a little upset; I have recently suffered the same affliction as yourself."

"What do you mean?" exclaimed Boy.

"I've been reduced," answered One-and-Nine sorrowfully. "You've been reduced too," he said, "but only in size. I've come down in price, which is far more serious. I was once Two-and-Three," he added regretfully.

"Oh! then you are the *other chap* that Pierrot sang about," said Boy, "and the Dolly-girl jilted you, didn't she, and——"

"That's not a matter of the slightest consequentiality," interrupted One-and-Nine; "she was a person of frivolaceous character, and though I am bound to admit that at one time I did devotionise her with considerable muchness, I have since found out that she was totally unworthy of my admirosity. Tin Soldier indeed!" he went on contemptuously, evidently referring to his rival, "why, he couldn't stand fire at all; he would melt! I don't deny that he looks very well on parade, but he would be no good in action. However, she has chosen to marry him and she must abide by the consequences. If people will marry *tin*, they must be prepared to find that it *melts*," he added sententiously.

"Oh! there's Sand Castle, I suppose!" cried Boy, as some lights appeared in the distance.

"Yes," replied One-and-Nine, "here we are!"

Boy could see when they reached the gates that it was the very Castle which he had so much admired in the morning. "And I am just the right size to go in, just as I wished to do," he thought glcefully.

A regiment of toy soldiers were drawn up before the gate and saluted as Boy and One-and-Nine entered.

Mr. and Mrs. Waxxe-Doll stood at the entrance to welcome their guests. Mrs. Waxxe-Doll was a very grand-looking personage in most fashionable attire, whilst her husband was not a wax doll at all, but a wooden and cardboard person with very thin, straight legs, and a large body and head which wobbled about when he was touched.

"So pleased to see you," said Mrs. Waxxe-Doll in a languid voice, shaking hands with Boy, and holding her hand nearly on a level with her head in doing so. "My husband," she said, introducing Boy, and then walking away.

"How do you do, sir?" said Boy, holding out his hand politely.

"What's that to do with you?" exclaimed Mr. Waxxe-Doll fiercely. "People have been asking me that silly question all the evening. Do you think I've got nothing better to do than stand here and answer foolish conundrums like that? I wonder you don't say it's a fine evening and have done with it! All the

other folks have been saying that too, one after the
other, like a lot of brainless lunatics. 'How do you
do? It's a fine evening!' Bah! If you haven't anything better to talk about than that, you had better
have stopped away!" And Mr. Waxxe-Doll glared at
Boy till he felt quite alarmed.

"Don't mind him," said One-and-Nine, "it's his way
—come along!" and he led the way into the Dancing
Hall where the festivities were in full swing. All kinds
of toys were represented, and it was indeed, as Pierrot
had said it would be, a very mixed gathering.

The guests were principally dolls dressed in the most
varied of costumes, from silks, brocades and satins, to
black paint; some fastidious-looking young gentlemen
with fair curled hair, and dressed in pale blue knitted
suits, were leaning against the wall in affected attitudes,
and a whole group of Dutch dolls were gathered around
a military-looking person in a cocked hat lolling
luxuriously on an ottoman at one end of the room.
There was a Toy Band at the other end, which looked
very imposing, but which Boy found out was only for
show, the Musicians only pretending to perform, while
the music was really supplied by a musical box hidden
away at the back. A number of dolls were dancing a

polka when Boy and One-and-Nine entered, so they sat down on a rout-seat near the door and watched them.

A supercilious-looking doll in evening dress sat next to Boy, fanning herself fussily.

"THE GUESTS WERE PRINCIPALLY DOLLS."

"Very mixed lot of people here," she began, without the slightest introduction. " I should not have come if I had known what to expect. Are you a friend of Mr. Waxxe-Doll's ?" she asked.

" No, I've never met him before," replied Boy.

"Ah! vulgar person, very—plenty of money, though —likes to be thought grand. Of course he isn't a Waxxe-Doll at all. His wife was a Waxxe and he took her name—it looks very well joined to his with a hyphen, you know. Mrs. Waxxe-Doll is of French descent, and gives herself airs in consequence. They've hired this Castle for the season at enormous expense, but bless you, they are nobodies! See that vulgar-looking old lady in the corner—with a pipe in her mouth—they call her Ancient Aunt Sarah; but she's nothing of the sort. Everybody knows her; she's just '*Old Aunt Sally, three-shies-a-penny*,' so it's no use their trying to disguise the fact. Look at those two," she went on, as two dolls in very straight narrow dresses danced past, "what guys! But there, what can you expect? They came out of the ark, I believe."

And Boy could see that they really did look like the figures out of Noah's Ark.

The music stopped just then, and most of the dolls went out into the grounds to get cool; and Boy, who did not at all care for the spiteful little person who had been letting him into all the Waxxe-Doll's family secrets, thought that he would follow their example.

One-and-Nine had wandered off by himself, so Boy had no one to talk to.

He found the grounds brilliantly illuminated with little wax vestas stuck in the sand, and the toy trees and rustic bridges looked quite pretty in the light. Three or four Gentlemen dolls were playing a kind of game by the pond, and asked Boy to join them. He found that it was called "Stock Brokers," and he soon learned how to play it.

Each had a large sheet of blue paper which was called a "Stock," and which when torn in half became a "Share." These pieces of paper were thrown into the air, and the game consisted in blowing under these pieces of paper, or "raising the wind," as it was called, in order to keep them floating: the one who kept his "Share" or "Stock" from falling longest won the game. Boy quite enjoyed playing it until one of his "Shares" fell to the ground, and then he was "broke," as they called it, and so he lost the game.

A crowd of dolls hurrying back to the Castle next attracted his attention, and, following them inside, he heard it announced that Sergeant One-and-Nine was about to recite. Boy was very glad to hear this, and

"ONE OF HIS 'SHARES' FELL TO THE GROUND."

managed to push forward to where One-and-Nine was standing.

The Master of Ceremonies was bustling about trying to find every one a seat; and at last, when the room was quite quiet, One-and-Nine began the following poem, which had been composed by himself:—

"THE MUS RIDICULOUS AND THE FELIS DOMESTICA.

"A Cat amidst the Burdock leaves
   Sat all disconsolate,
And sadsomely did wop and wole
   And role agaiust her fate.

"'Ah! hollow, hollow,' wole the Cat,
   'Is all Societee,
And falshish shamiosity
   In all around I see.'

"'Oh! why,' I crew in sympathy,
   'Lamentuate like that?
Pray tell me all your sorrowness';
   And down I flumply sat.

"The Cat did then all sobbishly
   Her woesome tale repeat.
'This world is full of mockishness,
   And also of deceit.

"'For why? This morn at dawnitude
   A mouse I did espy;
'Twas running whirligigishly
   Beneath my very eye.

'And feeling somewhat breakfastish
  I straightway gave a spring,
And landed right upon the back
  Of that activeous thing.

" ' To my surprise it did not squeak,
    And neither did it squeal;
And as 'twas rather littleish,
    I ate it at one meal.

" ' I much regret my hastiness,
    For soon, to my dismay,
'Twas acting most unmouseishly,
    In an eccentric way.

" ' 'Twas what they term a *clockwork* mouse,
    And governed by a spring;
Its works behaved revolvingly,
    And hurt like anything.

" 'Oh! tell me, is life livable
    When things go on like that?
When clockwork mice and feathered shams
    Impose upon a Cat?'

" I could not answer her, and so
    I softly snoke away;
I felt that 'twould be synicish
    To wish that Cat ' Good-day.' "

All the company applauded vigorously at the conclu-
sion of the recitation; and whilst the clapping was still
going on a black indiarubber doll rushed in with a very
scared face and cried out, "The tide is coming in!"

and there was immediately a great commotion throughout the room.

The company rushed helter-skelter to the gate, where they could see that the tide had indeed risen so high as to cut off all communication with the shore. Mr. Waxxe-Doll was stamping about in fury.

"See what comes of all this tomfoolery! Parties, indeed! and hiring Sand Castles for a lot of scatter-brains to make idiots of themselves in! Wait till I get safely home again on my shelf, and you don't catch me giving any more parties, I can tell you."

The remainder of the dolls were rushing madly about, wringing their hands and crying that they should all be drowned. One-and-Nine seemed to be the only person able to suggest anything.

"Here is a plank," he said, pointing to one which had been left on the sand; "we had better all get on to it, and the tide will carry us back to the shore."

The proposal was hailed with delight by the rest, and they all scrambled on to the plank and waited events. The elaborately dressed dolls in silk and satin held up their dainty skirts so that they should not get wet; whilst the Dutch dolls sat in a row on the edge of the plank with their legs dangling over the side.

Ancient Aunt Sarah threw conventionality to the winds, and lighted up her pipe, at which Mrs. Waxxe-Doll was so shocked that in her agitation she dropped her fan over the side of the plank.

Boy very politely jumped down to fetch it for her, and as he was stepping back a huge wave came rolling up

"SCRAMBLED ON TO THE PLANK AND WAITED EVENTS."

and carried off the plank with all the dolls on it, wetting Boy through to the skin and leaving him standing alone on the wet sand. As the plank with its cargo of screaming dolls floated away, One-and-Nine shouted out, "I will meet you again at Zum," just as they disappeared behind a rock standing out of the sea.

CHAPTER III.

PROFESSOR CRAB.

"GOOD gracious! whatever am I to do now?" thought Boy, for the tide was rising higher and higher every moment, and there seemed to be no possible way of getting back to the shore again. He had just decided to return to Sand Castle and see if he could not find something to make a raft of when he noticed a very large Crab in a white waistcoat and dark blue coat carrying a gold-headed cane in one claw, and walking rapidly towards him.

As soon as he perceived Boy he exclaimed in a delighted voice,—

"Why! Bless me, what a charming little human creature! How do you do, my dear sir?"

Boy, staring at him in great surprise, replied that he

was "quite well, thank you," and was just going to ask the Crab if he could suggest a way back to the shore, when a great wave rolled up unexpectedly and carried Boy and the Crab off their feet, destroying about half of Sand Castle, and washing away most of the toy trees which were in the garden.

"Very refreshing, sir, isn't it?" remarked the Crab, smoothing down his coat as the wave receded, leaving them on the wet sand.

Boy, drenched to the skin, was spluttering and gasping for breath, and could not reply for a moment or two, but at last he managed to say, "I think it is horrid, and I am sure I shall be drowned soon if this sort of thing goes on much longer. Do you know how I can get back to the shore?" he panted.

"You can't get back," said the Crab decidedly.

"Oh dear me! then I shall certainly be drowned!" cried Boy in alarm.

"What nonsense!" remarked the Crab. "That's what all the human creatures say directly they get a little wet. It's all affectation, my dear sir, I assure you. Why, look at me. I'm just as comfortable in the water as out of it, and so would you be if you would only try it. Here comes another wave. Now don't be frightened and don't let yourself be carried away; just stop on the sand and let the water go over you— give me your claw ;" and grasping Boy's hand he held him down while the wave passed over their heads. For a moment Boy could not breathe, but presently having swallowed a great mouthful of salt water, he found to his great surprise that he could breathe just as well under the water as out of it.

"There, what did I tell you?" remarked the Crab pleasantly, when Boy had partially recovered from his fright ; for there is no disguising the fact that he had been frightened, although he was a brave little fellow, too. "Come along," continued the Crab, "you had better come and see my school now you have got so far."

"Your school!" exclaimed Boy. "Do you keep a school?"

"Yes," replied the Crab, "I am the Head Master of Drinkon College."

"What a funny name!" said Boy smilingly.

"Not at all," replied the Crab; "no funnier than Eaton—Eaton on land and Drinkon under the sea, you know."

Boy thought about this as they proceeded along

the hard sand under the water, and then he noticed to his great surprise a number of fishes about his own size, in short jackets and deep collars, and wearing College caps, swimming in their direction.

"These are some of my scholars," remarked the Crab as they came in sight—the fishes, swimming in a perfectly upright position, raised their caps when they saw the Crab, and one of them said very politely,—

"Good-morning, Professor."

"Good-morning," replied the Crab as they swam past. Just then a curious-looking little creature covered all over with little prickly spikes called out rudely,—

"Yah! old Professor Crab—who caned the Oyster?" and scuttled away behind some seaweed.

"That," said the Crab, "is one of the Sea Urchins; they are very rude and ill behaved. I do not allow my scholars to associate with them."

"Are you really a Professor?" asked Boy, who felt greatly impressed with the Crab's importance.

"I'm afraid I am," said the Crab. "All schoolmasters are, you know—whether they admit it or not."

What do you mean?" exclaimed Boy. "I don't

think my schoolmaster is a Professor; at any rate he does not call himself one."

"Ah, that's his artfulness," said the Crab. "A professor," he explained, "is one who professes to know more than he really does, and all schoolmasters do that

" 'THESE ARE SOME OF MY SCHOLARS.' "

more or less, whether they admit it or not—they are obliged to; however, let's change the subject; it is a painful one."

Boy was greatly surprised at this admission on the part of the Crab, but he was too much interested in his strange surroundings to think much about it.

They were walking along a roadway with great seaweeds planted at regular intervals on either side, and in the distance Boy could see the outlines of some great buildings.

"Why, there are some houses!" he exclaimed in surprise.

"Of course," replied Professor Crab. "What did you suppose we lived in?"

"I had no idea that fishes built houses before," said Boy, "except sticklebacks; I know they build a kind of nest with sticks and things, because I have seen pictures of them in my Natural History book."

"My dear sir," remarked the Professor, "those were in the old days, before fishes became civilised: you might as well refer to the time when human creatures dwelt in caves and huts. No, my dear sir, the spread of education has extended to us also, and we have now as fine cities under the sea as any on land."

Boy was just going to reply when his attention was attracted by a party of Lobsters on bicycles rushing past them, all dressed alike in dark green and yellow. One dear little one riding along gallantly at the end of the procession amused Boy very much indeed, and he was still watching him when he heard a voice exclaiming, "Cab, sir?" and, turning around, beheld the

"'CAB, SIR?'"

most curious vehicle you can possibly imagine : two
sea-horses were attached to a kind of carriage made
out of a large shell mounted on two wheels, and were
driven by a small crayfish, wearing a top hat, who was
perched up behind.

"Yes, I think we will ride," said Professor Crab,
mounting the steps of this strange conveyance, and
beckoning Boy to follow. Boy was delighted to do so,
and was charmed with the curious little carriage as the
coachman cracked his whip and they bowled quickly
along. Presently they passed a large building looking
like a Station, and Professor Crab told him that it was
the Terminus of the Submarine Steam Navigation Company, and told the cabman to stop a moment so that
Boy might watch one of the boats which was just
starting out of the Station. A very curious affair it
turned out to be : shaped like an enormous Cigar, with a
screw propeller at one end of it ; a deck on top with rails
around it, on which a number of various kinds of fishes
were sitting about on deck-chairs, chatting and reading,
while through the large plate-glass windows, of which
there was one on either side of this curiously-shaped
boat, Boy could see a number of other fishes making
themselves comfortable in the luxuriously furnished

saloon. As soon as it floated away out of sight the cabman whipped up his horses again, and off they started once more, and did not stop until they reached some large gates with a board over them, on which was painted in gold letters :

DRINKON COLLEGE,

PRINCIPAL: PROFESSOR CRAB.

The Professor paid the cabman, who touched his hat, and then, followed by Boy, entered a large building just through the gates. A long corridor ran right through the building, and through the glass doors at the end Boy could see a number of the scholars at play.

"Would you like to join them while I give the First Class in Molluscs their singing lesson?" asked the Professor.

Boy said that he should, and passing out into the playground, was soon surrounded by a number of young fishes, all dressed in College suits similar to those Boy had seen before.

"What's your name?" asked one, as soon as he came up to Boy, and before he could answer another one had asked, "What's your father? and how much pocket money do you have a week?" while a third demanded, "Where did you go for your holiday last year?"

Boy thought he had better answer one question at a time, so he replied, "Oh, I went to Broadstairs and had such a jolly time, and one day I went out in a boat and caught such a lot of—— " (Fortunately he remembered just in time to prevent himself from saying "such a lot of fish" as he had at first intended.)

"Such a lot of what?" asked one of the little fishes curiously.

"Oh—cr—cr—such a lot of—cr—cr—things, shells, you know, and cr—cr—seaweed," stammered Boy, feeling very confused.

"Rather funny to go out in a boat to catch seaweed, wasn't it?" remarked one of the fishes suspiciously. "What did you catch really?"

Boy could not think what to say, but at last he thought that he could see a way out of the difficulty, and said, "Oh, I caught a crab."

The fishes looked horrified.

"Oh! I don't mean a really truly crab," Boy hastened to say. "I mean when your oars stick in the water and you can't draw them out again; that's called 'catching a crab,' you know, and that's the kind I mean, of course."

The fishes did not seem quite satisfied though, and stood staring at him suspiciously for some time, till at last one of them said,—

"Can you play cricket?"

"Yes, rather," said Boy proudly. "I'm going to be captain of our eleven next term if Traddles doesn't come back again."

"Who's Traddles?" demanded one of the fishes.

"Oh! a fellow at our school," said Boy. "He's eleven and ever so much taller than me; but I can bowl better than him any day."

"Come on then, let's have a game," said one of the fishes, leading the way to the end of the playground where a single wicket was pitched.

"Your innings," he cried, handing Boy a bat.

Boy thought this was a very curious way of beginning a game, and he was more surprised still when, without the slightest warning, all the rest of the fishes began throwing balls at him as hard as they could, hitting him pretty sharply in several places, and of course knocking the bails off the stumps at once.

"How's that, Umpire?" they shouted all together.

The fish who had handed Boy the bat promptly replied "Out," and the others threw their caps up into the air excitedly and called out that they had won the game.

"That's not the way to play cricket," cried Boy, throwing down his bat in disgust.

"Who says it isn't?" demanded one of the fishes, coming up to him.

"I say so," maintained Boy stoutly.

"Very well, then I'll fight you for it," declared the fish, throwing off his coat.

"I'm sure you won't," said Boy, laughing at the very idea.

"Yah! cowardy, cowardy custard," cried the fishes, dancing around him. "Afraid to fight; dear little mammy's baby."

Boy very wisely determined not to heed their taunts and walked back to the College, leaving the quarrelsome little fishes to themselves.

The sound of music from one of the class-rooms told him where he should find the Professor, and looking in at the window he saw the Crab standing beside a blackboard with notes on it waving a *bâton*, while a number of Oysters in rows were singing with their shells wide open.

The Missing Prince.

"Come in," he cried, when he saw Boy, and Boy went round to the door and entered the room.

"We have nearly finished," said Professor Crab. "Perhaps you would like to hear the Molluscs sing."

"Very much indeed," said Boy, taking a seat on one of the forms.

The Crab counted "One, two, three," beating time with his *bâton*, and the Oysters started singing the following song :—

"THE DEAR LITTLE OYSTER."

"There was once a little Oyster, living underneath the sea,
Who was good as gold and, consequently, happy as could be;
She kept the house as tidy and as clean as a new pin,
And helped her Ma to make the beds they tuck the Oysters in.

"We soon discovered she possessed a most uncommon voice,
And Operatic singing then became her ardent choice;
So diligently practised she her lessons and her scales,
That she quickly gained the medal given by the Prince of
Whales.

"Of course she now was far too good to waste her life down
here,
So reluctantly we gave her up to grace another sphere:
She, in a barrel nicely packed, was sent to Mr. Gatti,
And under his most skilful care became an Oyster Patti."

Boy was very pleased indeed with this song, which the First Class in Molluscs sang very well, and clapped vigorously.

"I'm glad you like their singing," said the Professor, looking pleased at Boy's approval.

"That will do for to-day," he added, dismissing the

"THE OYSTERS STARTED SINGING.

class, and the Oysters went out of the room in single file, each one making a little bow as he passed the Professor.

"Now what shall we do with ourselves for the rest of the day?" said the Crab, when they had all gone, "for there is a half-holiday, you know. Would you like to go for a trip to Zum?" he asked.

"Oh yes, please," answered Boy, who remembered that

that was where One-and-Nine said that they should meet again.

So Professor Crab put his hat on, and after locking the class-room door set out with Boy for the Station of the Submarine Navigation Company.

CHAPTER IV.

M.D. AND THE DOCTOR'S BILL.

HEY found a boat waiting when they reached the Station, and Professor Crab having purchased the tickets they went on board the singular conveyance. They had hardly taken their seats amongst a number of respectably dressed fishes when the bell rang and they were off.

Before they had proceeded far, Boy noticed a sudden rush to the great window at one side of the boat, and joining the crowd he heard some one say, "There goes the Prince of Whales."

Looking eagerly out of the window, he saw a whale very nicely dressed in a perfectly-fitting frock-coat and wearing a beautifully glossy new top hat; he had a gold-headed umbrella tucked under one

47

fin, and was followed by a crowd of small fishes who were evidently trying to attract his attention, but of whom he was not taking the slightest notice. He raised his hat, though, and bowed very affably as the crowd on the boat cheered him.

"His Marine Highness is looking very well, isn't he?" inquired a gentlemanly-looking Whiting of Boy, as the Prince of Whales disappeared from view.

"Very well indeed," replied Boy; "he seems to be very popular," he added.

"Oh yes, he is," replied the Whiting. "He is a capital fellow, and does an immense amount of good. He is on his way now to open the New Home for Distressed Barnacles, I believe."

An American King Crab, sitting near, remarked in a loud voice that he "didn't believe in Princes." "I guess we can do without them on our side of the herring pond," he said contemptuously, and then went over to speak to a small Oyster who was sitting the other side of the boat. Boy was rather interested in the King Crab, never having seen one of these curious-looking creatures before, so he walked over too, just in time to hear him say to the Oyster,—

"Native of these parts, I presume, stranger?"

The Oyster bowed.

"Wal, no offence to you, but I guess we've got Oysters over our side of the Atlantic that could knock you into fits. Why, we've got 'em so big over there that it takes two men and a boy to swallow one of them."

"I've heard my Uncle say," remarked Boy pleasantly, "that most things in America are on a very large scale; I suppose he must have been thinking of those oysters."

"Yes, Siree, I guess your Uncle's right. I reckon that our country is going to lick creation before long," said the American King Crab, walking away and looking very pleased.

"There, now you've made him happy," said the Oyster, laughing.

"Why, what have I done?" asked Boy innocently.

"Why, Americans are always very glad to hear their country praised, you know," said the Oyster; "let's come on deck and hear the singing."

Boy very readily followed him on to the deck where they found a crowd gathered around a couple of Soles with black faces, dressed in nigger costumes, who were singing to the accompaniment of a guitar the following song :—

"THE GREAT SEA SERPENT.

" I will sing a funny song
Of a serpent of the sea,
Which the sailors all declare
They have often seen disporting,
As they sailed in foreign parts,
Here and there and everywhere.

" And when editors of papers
Have no other news than this,
They will always find a space
For the story of a Captain,
A Lieutenant, or a Mate,
How this Monster they did face.

" And these stories vary strangely,
As such stories ofttimes do,
And they none of them agree
As to length, or the appearance,
Or in details such as these,
Of this Creature of the Sea.

" Some declare it's 'very lengthy,'
Others say it's 'rather short,'
And a Captain from the South
Says he saw it quite distinctly
With a schooner fully rigged
Disappearing down its mouth.

" Oh ! it's 'somewhat like a Camel,'
Or it's 'very like a Whale ; '

But the truth I now will sing:
It's like that Mrs. Harris
Mr. Dickens wrote about,
There *'was never no sich thing.'* ".

Great applause followed the singing and presently some one called out, " Sing the Alphabet song."

" Yes, yes," cried several fishes at once, " Alphabet song, Alphabet song."

So the two Soles bowed and commenced as follows :—

"ALPHABETICUS.

"One day *A* Cockney, who shall *B*
The hero of our song,
Went out an Irish friend to *C*
And said he'd not be long.

"This friend lived by the River *D*;
Although an Irishman,
He laughed with glee his friend to see,
And thus their converse ran:

"'Bedad, how are ye?' with a bow,
Said Paddy, quite a swell;
The Cockney said, ''*E* 'oped as 'ow
The Irishman wus well.'

"'Quite well, and *F* ye'll come wid me
I'd think it kind; for why?
I'm going to Town on my *G*-gee
A large *H* bone to buy.'

The Missing Prince.

" 'My friend, *I* will, upon my word'
The Cockney then did say,
'I'll come with you just like a bird—
A bird they call a *J.*'

"'Come, thin,' said Pat, 'no longer wait,
We're losing half the day;
And sure thin since we may be late
We'd better take the *K.*'

"And as they to the town did go,
'Twas thus the Cockney spake:
I'll buy an *L* of calico
Some handkerchiefs to make.'

" 'My wife can *M* them, then you know
I'll buy such things as these—
An old brown *N*, and perhaps an '*O*,
To hoe our beans and *P*'s.

" 'And if we pass a Barber's there,
I've really half a mind
To have my hair, I do declare,
Done in a *Q* behind.'

"'Bedad t'would suit you fine,' said Pat;
'I'll have mine done as well.
You *R* a brick to think of that!
Oh! sha'n't I look a swell!'

"Their shopping took the whole day through
There was so much to see;

Then Paddy said 'Allow me to
*S*cort you home to *T*.

"'And *U* and I by hook or crook
On good things shall be fed.'
And, like Sam Weller in the book,
' *V* vill,' the Cockney said.

" They had their tea, then Paddy spoke:
'I feel in merry case.
Shall I tell you a funny joke,
And pull a funny face

"'To *W* with laughter up
And stand upon my head?'
' *X*actly so,' the Cockney cried,
' *Y*, certainly,' he *Z*."

Quite a crowd of fishes had gathered round the two Soles while they were singing this song, and after it was all over one of them went round with his hat and collected pennies just as the real niggers do. Boy noticed while this was going on that the boat was gradually rising to the surface of the sea, and presently he found that the deck was above the water and that he was breathing air again. He could see that they were approaching a Quay with a number of very quaint, old-fashioned buildings beyond it. A great crowd of people were gathered close to the edge of the Quay, and were pointing excitedly at something in the water, and as the boat drew nearer to the shore Boy could hear a number of directions being shouted at once.

" Throw him a rope."

" Nonsense !   He is insensible, and wouldn't see it."

" Well, you swim out to him then."

" Sha'n't !   Do it yourself."

" Throw stones at him and try and float him ashore that way."

This last direction seemed to find most favour, and everybody began throwing stones at the object, whatever it was, in the water.

The boat had now come quite close to the Quay, and Boy could see that it was poor One-and-Nine who was attracting all this attention. He was floating on the top of the water with his eyes shut and half the paint washed off one side of his head He looked the picture of misery, but Boy was very glad to find that he was still alive, for he opened his eyes and feebly cried, " Don't throw with such hardness," whenever a stone accidentally hit him, which was very frequently, for you see there were such a number of people throwing them Boy felt very sorry for his old companion,

and as soon as the boat reached the Quay he ran
ashore and hurried to the place where they were trying
to land the poor Wooden Soldier.

They had just succeeded in dragging him ashore
with a boat-hook when Boy reached the crowd, and a

"'THROW STONES AT HIM.'"

fussy little gentleman was telling the people to "stand
back and give him air."

"Who is that gentleman?" asked Boy of one of the
crowd standing near him.

"Why, the M.D., of course," was the reply.

Boy being still in doubt ventured to ask what
these letters stood for, and was informed that they
stood for Mad Doctor. "All doctors are mad, you

know," said his informant ; "that's why they are obliged to put those letters after their names."

Boy had never heard of this before, though he had often wondered what the letters meant. He tried to get nearer to One-and-Nine, and just caught a glimpse of the M.D. bending over him, and heard the Wooden Soldier explaining something about "The wet-ness of the water."

"Yes, yes, my poor fellow," the M.D. was saying. "Don't try to talk. Has he any friends here?" he asked, looking round.

"Yes," cried Boy, "I know him," and the crowd immediately parted and made way for him to get nearer.

"Ah!" said the M.D., looking at Boy over the top of his gold-rimmed glasses. "There's. nothing much the matter with him except a slight attack of 'Water on the grain ;'" and the M.D. passed his hand over the Wooden Soldier's head where the paint was washed off. "A little Enamel will soon set that right; go and fetch some," he continued, turning to a small boy in buttons standing near him. The boy hurried off and soon returned, bearing a large tin of green Enamel and a brush. Boy looked at him in amazement when

"BEGAN TO PAINT THE SIDE OF ONE-AND-NINE'S HEAD GREEN."

he came back, for he seemed to have grown several inches taller in the few minutes that he had been away. No one else, though, seemed to have noticed it, and the M.D. took the brush and began to paint the side of One-and-Nine's head green.

The Wooden Soldier sighed once or twice, and then sat up and looked around him.

"Well, my man, how do you feel now?" said the M.D. kindly.

"Oh, a little much more better, thank you," said One-and-Nine faintly. "That's not a colour of much fashionableness, though, is it?" he asked, looking at the green Enamel dubiously.

"It's a most uncommon colour for the hair," said the M.D., daubing another patch at the back of his head, "and will go beautifully with your red tunic. There, that will do nicely; take the paint away, Bill," he said to the page-boy.

"Very well, sir," answered a voice a long way up in the air, and turning round, Boy could see that Bill, as he was called, had grown about twice as tall as he was before. His master did not seem at all surprised, however, and sent him off with the paint.

"And take that medicine to the Lord High Fiddle-de-dee's as soon as you get back," he called out as the boy hurried off, "and say he's to be well shaken before they give it to him."

The crowd was beginning to disperse, and One-and-Nine seemed to be all right again, although Boy thought that he looked rather peculiar with part of his head painted green.

"Which way are you going?" asked the M.D., smiling kindly at Boy.

"Oh! back to the boat again, I think," answered Boy; but when he turned to the Quay he found that the boat had disappeared.

"Why, it's gone!" he cried.

"Oh yes," said the M.D., "it only stays here for a few moments; "you had better come with me," he suggested kindly.

Boy thought that they might as well do that as anything else, so One-and-Nine and he followed the M.D. through the quaint street with the curious old houses.

"There's my Bronchitis," cried the M.D. suddenly, pointing to a large house on the right, "and there's my Sciatica opposite; I have a Whooping Cough in

the next street, and the Measles a little further on,"
he added proudly.

Boy looked around in alarm, wondering whatever the
M.D. meant.

"Oh, here comes my Lumbago," he cried, as an old
gentleman walking with crutches came hobbling along
the street, and then Boy could see that he had been
referring to his patients.

The M.D. stopped to speak to his Lumbago, and Boy
could see the page-boy, taller than ever, hurrying down
the street with a basket on his arm containing some
medicine-bottles.

"That boy grows very quickly," said Boy to One-
and-Nine while they were waiting for the M.D.

"Doctors' Bills always do," said One-and-Nine un-
concernedly; "that's how the Doctors live, you know."

"What do you mean?" exclaimed Boy.

"Why, when a Doctor's Bill grows too long, his
patients pay him to get a shorter one—that's how it
is that M.D.'s change their boys with such frequent-
ness."

"What a lot of things I am learning to-day, to
be sure," thought Boy as the M.D. came back to
them.

"Most interesting case," he declared, evidently referring to the old gentleman whom he had just left. "The Lumbago is turning to Haberdashery in the left leg." Then seeing that Boy looked very puzzled he added, "That's the scientific name for 'Pins and Needles,' you know."

"Oh!" said Boy. "Have you very many patients?" he asked.

"Oh yes," said the M.D., smiling happily; "this is a most delightfully unhealthy spot. Good gracious," he continued, "there's that boy fighting again." And the M.D. strode forward to where a small crowd was gathered round the Doctor's Bill and another boy, who were fighting desperately. The M.D. rushed between them, and giving his boy a sharp box on the ears, asked him "what he meant by fighting with a common Grocer's Bill."

"It's most unseemly," he went on, "for you to be continually quarrelling with Tradesmen's Bills: remember you have a position to keep up, and if you must fight, never let me catch you doing so again with any one less than a Lawyer's Bill at least."

"Please, sir," blubbered the Doctor's Bill, "there

isn't a Lawyer's Bill my size in the kingdom; the shortest one is twice as long as I am."

"Very well, then, don't fight at all," said the M.D. severely, and the Doctor's Bill walked away sniffing

"'I MUST LEAVE YOU NOW.'"

and sobbing with the basket on his arm, while the Grocer's Bill stood a little way off making grimaces at him.

"These Bills are a great nuisance," said the M.D.,

"and are continually quarrelling; but I must leave you now, for I have to visit the Lord High Fiddle-de-dee, who is suffering with Gout. Good-day," and he hurried up the stone steps of a handsome building on the opposite side of the street.

CHAPTER V.

THE COUNCILLORS OF ZUM.

WHY, here he comes" exclaimed the M.D., as a very tall, aristocratic-looking gentleman opened the door and walked hurriedly down the steps.

"My dear sir, this is really too bad ; you mustn't think of going out, ill as you are," he said.

"Oh, nonsense, my dear M.D.," said the Lord High Fiddle-de-dee. "State matters of the utmost importance demand my immediate attendance at the House of Words, and I must go whether I am well or not. Who are these persons with you?" he continued, staring rather hard at Boy and One-and-Nine.

"Oh ! I really don't know their names," replied

the M.D. " I think they are respectable persons, though."

" Have they a vote ? " inquired the Lord High Fiddle-de-dee anxiously.

" Yes, I think so," said the M.D., referring to his watch. " They have been in the Town over an hour."

" Oh, that's all right, then," said the Lord High Fiddle-de-dee ; " every one who has lived here for more than an hour is entitled to a vote. Bring them along ; they may be useful. What's your name ? " he continued, turning to Boy.

" My name is Cyril, but I am usually called Boy," was the reply.

" And yours ? " asked the Lord High Fiddle-de-dee of the Wooden Soldier.

" One-and-Nine, Your Honour," replied he, saluting respectfully.

" Rubbish, I didn't ask your price," said the Lord High Fiddle-de-dee impatiently. " I want to know your name."

" One-and-Nine, Your Honour," repeated the Wooden Soldier.

The Lord High Fiddle-de-dee stared at him for a moment, and then turned to M.D. and said, " Is this

man a little—— and he tapped his forehead in-
quiringly.

"Yes; softening of the grain," replied the M.D.,
nodding.

"Ah, I thought so," remarked the Lord High Fiddle-
de-dee. "Never mind, bring him along; even lunatics
can vote here, you know," and linking his arm in that
of the M.D. they proceeded down the street, followed
by Boy and One-and-Nine.

"He is a person of great dignitude, evidently,"
whispered the Wooden Soldier, who was apparently
greatly impressed by the Lord High Fiddle-de-dee's
aristocratic bearing. "And although he is rather abrupteous in his manner, I think I admirationise him, don't
you?"

"Yes. He seems to be a very nice gentleman," agreed
Boy. "I wonder what we shall see and hear at the
House of Words? Oh! I suppose this is it," he continued, as they turned a corner, and an imposing-looking
building surrounded by an excited crowd of people
came in sight.

The Lord High Fiddle-de-dee seemed to be a very
well-known personage, and the crowd respectfully divided
and allowed them to pass through to the entrance of

the building, where an attendant opened the door and showed them along a corrider to another door marked Committee Room, which the Lord High Fiddle-de-dee opened and they all passed in.

A number of grandly dressed individuals were walking about, or chatting in little groups as they entered.

" Oh ! here comes the Lord High Fiddle-de-dee," cried some one directly they were inside the door. " Any news ? " he inquired anxiously.

The Lord High Fiddle-de-dee shook his head sadly.

" Well, we are all here now, so we had better proceed to business ; take your seats, please, gentlemen," said a very important-looking gentleman in a red gown and wig, seated at the head of a long table on which were pens and paper arranged neatly before each chair.

" Members of the Committee will please take their seats in the following order of precedence," drawled a melancholy voice from a desk at the further end of the room, where a worried-looking little old man, in a very rusty black gown, and who wore enormous green goggles, sat with a large book open before him, and a quill pen stuck behind his ear :—

" The King's Exaggerator," he called out ;

" The Lord High Fiddle-de-dee;

" The First Lord of the Cash Box ;

" The Advertiser General ;

" The Minister of Experiments ;

" The Public Persecutor ;

" The Busybody Extraordinary ;

" The Gentleman of the Glove Box ;

" The First Groom of the Boot Brushes ;

" The Kitchen Poker in Waiting ; and

" His Insignificance the Court Poet.

" Other persons to sit where they can."

As each one of these names was called out one of
the gentlemen sat down, so that Boy was able to tell
exactly who they were ; and as all the seats at the table
were now occupied, the M.D., One-and-Nine, and Boy
found seats against the wall near the Clerk who had
called out the names.

As soon as they were seated, the old gentleman got
out of his box and shuffled forward with some paper, a
pot of ink and some pens. These he put into Boy's
hands and muttered something about " fetching a
table."

" What are these for ? " inquired Boy.

" Paper for your impressions," drawled the Clerk. " I

suppose you have come to report this meeting, haven't you?"

"No, indeed I haven't!" said Boy in alarm.

"Dear me! What have you come for then?" asked the old Clerk in an amazed voice.

"Hush! hush!" called out some one, "His Importance is about to speak," and the old Clerk hobbled back to his seat, looking more worried than ever, while the gentleman seated at the head of the table, and who Boy found was called The Lord High Adjudicator, arose and made the following speech :—

"Gentlemen, we are met for the purpose of discussing the grave situation caused by the extraordinary absence of His Serene Importance the Crown Prince of Zum——"

"Hereditary Grand Duke of Grumbleberry Plumbhop, Knight of the Order of——" began the King's Exaggerator, when he was interrupted by the Public Persecutor, who inquired,—

"What's the use of all that, when there is no one but us to hear you?"

"I must perform my official duties," remarked the King's Exaggerator.

"You can have no official duties now that there is

no King and the Prince has disappeared," objected the Public Persecutor.

"Gentlemen, gentlemen, pray don't argue," interrupted the Lord High Adjudicator, "or we shall waste all day in discussion. If the King's Exaggerator wishes to do

"THE OLD GENTLEMAN . . . SHUFFLED FORWARD WITH SOME PAPER."

a little exaggerating on his own account, I am sure no one will object, but he must do it outside and not here; and now, in order that you may understand it all more clearly, I will call upon His Insignificance the Court Poet to read us "The Cause of Dismay."

The Court Poet, who was a very curious-looking man,

was dressed in a tightly-fitting velvet costume with a deep lace collar, and wore his hair very long. He had most prominent eyes, which he rolled about in a grotesque way as he spoke. When thus called upon he arose, and tragically clutching his hair with one hand, he waved the other about frantically, while he began in a shrill voice:—

> "THE CAUSE OF DISMAY.
>
> "Oh, men of Zum, what shall we do?
>   Our King has no successor;
> The Prince has vanished from our view,
>   And—and——"

"Well, go on!" shouted several voices.

> "vanished from our view,
>   And—and——"

repeated the Court Poet, turning very pale.

"Why don't you proceed?" inquired the Lord High Adjudicator.

"I'm afraid I can't find a rhyme for successor," admitted the Court Poet, looking greatly confused.

"Dear me! this is the second time this week you have failed in your rhyming," exclaimed the Lord High Adjudicator impatiently. "It's most annoying."

"It's unbearable," declared the Public Persecutor.

"WHY DON'T YOU PROCEED?" INQUIRED THE LORD HIGH ADJUDICATOR."

"If he can't do his work properly, we had better reduce his salary," suggested the Busybody Extra-ordinary.

"Hear, hear!" shouted several voices at once.

"Oh, please don't!" pleaded the Court Poet. "My stipend is very small as it is."

"Six pounds a year is a great deal more than you are worth!" declared the First Lord of the Cash Box emphatically.

"So it is, so it is!" agreed the rest of the Committee.

The poor Court Poet looked very crestfallen, while the two gentlemen sitting near him frowned at him severely, the Kitchen Poker in Waiting looking particularly disgusted.

"Ahem! I should like to suggest," said the Minister of Experiments, coughing importantly and standing up to address the meeting, "that instead of reducing his salary we should reduce his title, and that, instead of his being known as His Insignificance the Court Poet, he should in future be called His Absolute Nothingness the Public Rhymester."

This proposal seemed to find favour with the whole company, and, being put to the vote, was carried unanimously; and His Absolute Nothingness the Public

Rhymester was told to sit down, which he did very meekly, looking half inclined to burst into tears.

" Now then," said the Lord Chief Adjudicator when this was all over, " we really must get to business ; and as the Public Rhymester is not capable of setting forth ' The Cause of Dismay' in verse, as is the custom here, I must try and explain to you in prose. The facts, as you are aware, are as follows: Our late Sovereign, King Robert the Twentieth——"

" King of Zum and Emperor of——" began the King's Exaggerator, evidently intending to enumerate all of the late King's titles ; but he was forcibly prevented from doing so by the two gentlemen sitting next to him, one of whom held him down, while the other tied a handkerchief tightly over his mouth.

The Lord High Adjudicator nodded approval and proceeded.

" Our late Sovereign, King Robert the Twentieth, being deceased, and the Crown Prince having mysteriously disappeared some five years since, and there being no legal successor to the throne, what are we to do for a King? As you are aware, this land has always been governed by a hereditary absolute Monarchy, and His late never-to-be-sufficiently-lamented Majesty left absolutely no

relations whatever ; what are we to do about the government of the country? That is the question, gentlemen,
which we have met here to discuss to-day."

Almost before the Lord High Adjudicator had finished,
every member of the Committee got up excitedly and
began to unfold his own particular plan for the government
of the land, each trying to drown the other's voice. The
noise was deafening, and the poor old Clerk was so
alarmed at the uproar, that he collapsed into his box
and was found after the meeting still sitting on the floor
with his fingers pressed to his ears and trembling with
fright.

For some time the utmost confusion reigned, but at
last the Lord High Adjudicator stood up in his chair
and motioned them all to sit down, which, after a time,
they did.

Gentlemen, gentlemen, this is disgraceful !" cried the
Lord High Adjudicator when order was somewhat restored. "We shall never get on at this rate. Now, one
at a time, please."

The Busybody Extraordinary at once got up and began
as follows : —

" I have been preparing a little scheme for the government of Zum, which is bound, I think, to meet with the

approval of every one here—it is so delightfully simple, and at the same time so effective. There is no King. Very good, *we* will govern the land ; we will form ourselves into a Council for the management of everybody's business in the kingdom, with the power to take over all property, public and private, have control of everything and everybody in the land. Think what a benefit it would be to the Public not to have to worry about anything at all, simply to do as we told them, and think how delightful it would be for us! "

" But would the Public agree to all this ? " inquired the Lord High Fiddle-de-dee dubiously.

" The Public," said the Busybody Extraordinary contemptuously, " will do just whatever we wish it to. It may grumble a little at first, but it will do it all the same."

" But what shall we be called ? " asked the Public Persecutor, who seemed greatly interested in the scheme.

" Well, I was going to propose that we should call ourselves Public Councillors," replied the Busybody Extraordinary. " Of course, we should have to give up our present Official Titles and simply use our ordinary names with the letters P.C. added. Thus I should be known as Ebenezer Smith, P.C., and you would be Sir Peter Grumble, P.C., and so on."

"But how would it be possible to manage everybody's affairs?" inquired another.

"My dear sir," replied the Busybody Extraordinary, "that is the great point of the whole system—it is as easy as A.B.C. We should of course begin by commanding that *nothing whatever should be done without our sanction;* that would simplify matters to start with. Then we should turn our attention to public improvements; for instance, we should begin by pulling down this building and erect for our use some fine Municipal Buildings on a very large and handsome scale, with portraits of ourselves painted on all the windows."

"But who would pay for them?" objected the First Lord of the Cash Box.

"The Public, of course," said the Busybody Extraordinary. "What a silly question!"

"But supposing they refused?" persisted the First Lord of the Cash Box.

"The Public refuse to pay rates and taxes?" exclaimed the Busybody Extraordinary. "Who ever heard of such a thing? Really, my dear sir, you are most childish in your remarks. Then," he continued, "we should pull down all those buildings opposite and make a wide, handsome road, with trees on either side, with a large park at the end of it, beautifully laid out with lakes, etc., where we could drive in the afternoon. Of course, it would have to be railed in or we should have the Public trespassing in it."

" Wouldn't the Public expect to be allowed to use the park if they paid for all these improvements ? " asked the Advertiser General.

" But they mustn't expect anything of the sort," said the Busybody Extraordinary impatiently.   " The Public must be taught not to question anything that we do.   It will never do for us to be hampered by mere Public opinion, you know ; besides, they would not have time to use the park if they wanted to, because they would all be at school."

" But not grown-up people, surely ! " exclaimed the First Gentleman of the Glove Box.

" Why not ? " retorted the Busybody Extraordinary. " It will keep them out of mischief, and I am sure some grown-up people require to go to school quite as much as the youngsters.   The gymnastic exercises will be so good for them, too—especially the old ones.   Why, I have known some old men of eighty, or even ninety, who positively didn't know how to turn a somersault.   Such ignorance is absolutely appalling.   And you must be aware that at the present time not more than one-third of the servant-girls of Zum can play the piano. We can't allow this sort of thing to go on, you know. Then there is too much liberty allowed the Public in the matter of pleasures and entertainments; an occasional tea-party or a spelling-bee ought to satisfy any reasonable Public, and we could insist that in the case of tea-parties a plan of the house should be sent us, and a list of all the invited guests submitted for our approval with their certificates of birth and vaccination. In this way we should gradually get the Public completely under our control, and would hear no more of such nonsense as their presuming to object to anything we chose to do." And the Busybody Extraordinary sat down triumphantly, but somewhat breathless, after this long speech.

"H'm! there seems to be a great deal to be said in favour of his scheme," said the Lord High Adjudicator thoughtfully.

"A most brilliant proposal," agreed the Public Persecutor enthusiastically.

"There is only one thing," said the Kitchen Poker in Waiting, getting up and addressing the Meeting generally, "that I should like to suggest, and that is, that instead of this proposed Public Council a King

6

should be elected from our number, and although I don't wish to boast, I feel sure that there is no one in the entire assembly who would fill the position more ably and with greater dignity than myself."

" 'TOLD ME TO BRING YEZ THIS BIT OF A LETTER.' "

"It's like your cheek!" exclaimed the First Groom of the Boot Brushes. "I should think if any one is elected King I ought to stand before you."

There was evidently going to be a squabble unless the Lord High Adjudicator interfered, and he had just arisen in his seat for that purpose when there was a knock at the door, and an attendant entered.

"Av ye plaze, yer honours, there's a woman and a bit of a child wanting to see yer honours on a mather of importance," he said.

"What nonsense!" exclaimed the Lord High Adjudicator. "Tell the woman that we are engaged."

"I did, yer honour," exclaimed the attendant, "and she wouldn't take the answer, but told me to bring yez this bit of a letter."

The Lord High Adjudicator took the note which the attendant handed him, and after reading a few lines jumped up excitedly.

"Show her in at once," he cried; and when the attendant had gone out of the room he announced, in a voice trembling with excitement: "She says that she has news of the Crown Prince."

CHAPTER VI.

MRS. MARTHA MATILDA NIMPKY.

HE Lord High Adjudicator had barely made this announcement when the attendant returned, followed by a rosy-cheeked woman in a very bright shawl and a bonnet with an enormous quantity of flowers and feathers on it. She had little black corkscrew curls hanging down on either side of her face, and was leading a little boy of about four years of age by the hand: he was very beautifully dressed, and was a charming little fellow with short golden curls and a chubby, little, smiling face.

The woman stopped at the door and made a curtsey, while the little boy looked about him with great curiosity.

"Mrs. Martha Matilda Nimpky, widow, gentlemen

announced the woman, "and His Little Royal Highness, the son of the Crown Prince of Zum."

"Bless me, my good lady, you don't say so!" said the Lord High Adjudicator, jumping up from his chair and offering it to the woman, while the Busybody Extraordinary fussed about and placed another chair by its side with his cloak over it to make it look something like a throne for His Little Royal Highness.

"Yes, gentlemen, I have a strange story indeed to tell you," said Mrs. Martha Matilda Nimpky when they had all settled down again.

"Before you begin, I should like to ask, is His Royal Highness the Crown Prince alive and well?" asked the Lord High Adjudicator anxiously.

"Well, I can hardly tell you, sir," replied Mrs. Martha Matilda Nimpky. "He's invisible."

"Invisible!" exclaimed everybody in surprise.

Mrs. Martha Matilda Nimpky nodded mysteriously, and drew the little Prince closer to her so that she could put one arm around him.

"The Crown Prince of Zum and his dear lady, who was the Princess of Limesia, have both been rendered invisible by the King of Limesia's Magician, Ohah!"

"Dear me, how very shocking!" exclaimed the Lord

High Adjudicator, while the rest of the Committee dis-
played the greatest of interest.

"Yes, gentlemen, it happened in this way," continued
Mrs. Martha Matilda Nimpky. "When your Crown
Prince started on his travels about five years ago, he
came to Limesia, and seeing our dear Princess, at once
fell in love with her and wished to marry her. The
King of Limesia, however, who was still angry about
that affair of the Portmanteau——"

"Yes, yes, we know about it," exclaimed the Lord
High Adjudicator, nodding violently.

"Well," continued Mrs. Martha Matilda Nimpky, "the
King of Limesia wouldn't hear of their getting married,
so as they were very much in love with each other they
were married secretly and lived in concealment until
about three months ago, when your King of Zum died
and the Prince thought that he ought to come home and
be crowned King. But before they started, he and the
Princess went to the King of Limesia to beg his for-
giveness. Instead of forgiving them, though, he flew
into a fearful passion, and summoning Ohah, the
Magician, he ordered him to cast a spell upon both of
them so that they might gradually become invisible.
Poor dears! I shall never forget that day when they

"'LOOKING VERY INDISTINCT ABOUT THE HEAD.'"

drove home from the Palace, looking very indistinct about the head, and told me what had happened; for you must understand I have been living with them ever since they were married, first as the dear Princess's Maid, then as Nurse to the dear little Prince here. Well, as I was saying, the Prince told me all about it. 'Nimpky,' he said—that was the way he always addressed me, gentlemen—' Nimpky, it will be useless now for me to go to Zum. I am quite sure that an invisible King would be a great trial to my poor subjects, and I feel more and more shadowy every hour. You must take the little Prince '—meaning this little lamb, gentlemen—' You must take the little Prince to Zum and tell the Lord High Adjudicator all about it, and give him this signet-ring, which he will recognise as having belonged to me, and see that the little Prince is made King, because he is the lawful successor to my father's throne.' Those were his very words, gentlemen, and soon after his head disappeared entirely, so that he was unable to speak. The poor dear Princess disappeared too, a bit at a time, and although for a day or two we could understand them a little by the signs which they made, they eventually became so indistinct that we could scarcely see them at all. The dear Princess's left foot was the last thing to go, and that remained visible for some days after the rest of her body had disappeared. People used to come from miles, I assure you, gentlemen, to see her Royal Highness's foot, for she was greatly beloved by all the people at Limesia, and now, out of respect for her, all the ladies have taken to going about with their feet bare like the Princess's; for I must tell you, gentlemen, that our Princess was noted for her beautiful feet, and had never worn shoes in her life, only sandals when she walked abroad. Poor dear! I often think there must have been something she wanted to tell me very much, by the way in which her big toe wriggled about just before the foot entirely disappeared, which was only ten days ago." And Mrs. Martha Matilda Nimpky put her handkerchief to her eyes.

"Well, gentlemen," she continued, after a time, "I waited until the last symptom of my dear Prince and Princess had vanished, and then I journeyed here to fulfil the Prince's wish. I had to be very careful about it too, for if that old King knew about the little Prince (which fortunately he does not) he would have caused him to have been made invisible too. Now there's one thing I should like to beg of you, gentlemen, and that is that you will allow me to continue to be Nurse to His Little Royal Highness, for I am greatly attached to the dear little fellow ;" and Mrs. Martha Matilda Nimpky took the little Prince on to her lap and lovingly brushed the little golden curls from his forehead.

"Dear me! dear me! this is a very extraordinary story," said the Lord High Adjudicator. "May I see the signet-ring, please?" he asked.

"Certainly, sir; here it is," replied Mrs. Martha Matilda Nimpky, handing him a very curiously wrought golden ring.

"Yes, that belonged to His Royal Highness, sure enough," declared the Lord High Adjudicator; "and now that I look more closely at the little boy I can see that he bears a remarkable likeness to the Crown Prince."

"Long live the King!" shouted the Busybody Extraordinary suddenly ; and everybody else got up and joined in the cry, "Long live the King! Long live the King!" till the rafters rang again.

The little Prince looked somewhat alarmed at all the shouting, but he was a brave little fellow, and only said to Mrs. Martha Matilda Nimpky,—

"Nurse, what do all those mans make that noise for?"

The Nurse said something to quiet him, and they all sat down again ; and then the Lord High Adjudicator, after conferring with some of the other gentlemen, said,—

" Mrs. Martha Matilda Nimpky, on behalf of the rest of the Committee and myself, I should like to say that we think you have behaved in a very praiseworthy manner in obeying His Invisible Highness' wishes so . carefully, and we shall be very glad indeed if you will accept the post of Grand Perpetual Nurse to the King of Zum (for of course His Royal Highness will be crowned to-morrow) at a suitable salary and a choice of apartments in the Royal Palace."

" Hear, hear ! " shouted several of the Committee, while the Kitchen Poker in Waiting foolishly started singing, " For she's a jolly good fellow," and was promptly suppressed.

" I shall be delighted, gentlemen, to accept 'the position ! " said Mrs. Martha Matilda Nimpky, looking greatly pleased.

" Then there is nothing further to be done but to conduct you to the Palace and to make preparations for His Royal Highness' Coronation to-morrow," said the Lord High Adjudicator, leading the way to the door.

The Royal Nurse took the Prince's hand, and was preparing to follow, when the little fellow caught sight of Boy, who had been sitting with One-and-Nine and the M.D. listening with the greatest attention to all that was going on.

"'WHO'S THAT BOY, NURSE?'"

"Who's that boy, Nurse?" asked the Prince.

"Hush, dear, I don't know," said the Royal Nurse.

"But I want him to come and play with me," demanded His Royal Highness, "and that Soldier man, too."

"My dear, you must be a good boy and come with

Nurse. Perhaps another day the little boy will be allowed to play with you," said the Royal Nurse, trying to lead him along.

" But I want him to come now, Nurse dear," persisted the little Prince.

" If His Royal Highness desires it," suggested the Busybody in Extraordinary, "you had better let the boy accompany you to the Palace. When His Royal Highness is made King to-morrow, you know, his wishes will have to be obeyed absolutely."

So Boy and One-and-Nine were told to follow the others into the Palace, which joined the House of Words, and which was a very magnificent place. A large crowd of Servants were in the Hall, and outside Boy could hear shouts of "Long live the King! Long live the King!" For the news of the little Prince's arrival had travelled quickly, and the people were all delighted to welcome a grandson of the late King, who had been greatly beloved, notwithstanding a very awkward circumstance about a Portmanteau, which, perhaps, I will tell you later on.

The little Prince and the Royal Nurse were conducted up the grand staircase, the Prince turning around to Boy and saying, " Good-night, little Boy, I'm sleepy tired now, but I shall see you to-morrow," while Boy and One-and-Nine were led in another direction to a suite of rooms overlooking a beautiful garden. Here they were served with a bountiful supper by a Footman, who had been set apart to wait upon them only. His name, Boy found out, was Cæsar Maximilian Augustus Claudius Smith, but he was called Thomas for short. Thomas was a very nice man, Boy thought, and although he seemed to think a great deal of himself he was very kind to them.

After they had finished supper and Thomas had cleared away the supper things, Boy noticed that One-and-Nine seemed very quiet.

" Is there anything the matter ? " he asked anxiously.

" I am afraid," remarked One-and-Nine sadly, " that she will never condescentionise to affectionate me."

" Who ? " exclaimed Boy.

" That majestuous lady, the Royal Nurse," said One-and-Nine, sighing sentimentally.

" You don't mean to say that you have fallen in love with her, surely ? " said Boy, feeling greatly inclined to laugh.

" Who could help it ? " declared the Wooden Soldier. " I am completely smot ! "

" Smot ! What's that ? " asked Boy.

Smite, smitten, smot," exclaimed One-and-Nine. "And what a charmaceous name, too," he continued— "Martha Matilda Nimpky. How lovelyish! Do you think she cares for me even a smallish bit ? "

" ' I AM COMPLETELY SMOT.' "

" Well, I'm afraid she scarcely saw you, you know," said Boy. " Perhaps she will when she knows you better," he added, wishing to comfort the poor lovesick soldier.

" Do you think it would be wise to send her a love-letter ? " asked One-and-Nine anxiously, " or an Ode," he suggested, brightening up. "Yes, I'll write her an Ode—that's what I'll do."

"I'm afraid I don't quite know what an Ode is," admitted Boy; "but I suppose it won't do any harm to send it."

"Oh, an Ode is a kind of Poemish letter that people send when they are in love. I've Oded before," said One-and-Nine, giggling foolishly.

"What shall you say?" inquired Boy.

"Well, let me see," said One-and-Nine. "In Oding a lady you have to think of what you most admire in her, and take that as your subject. The last time I Oded, you know, it was about Miss Dolly-girl's eyes. It began thusly:

> "'The Rose is red, the Violet's blue,
> But neither have such eyes as you.
> Yours are the kind I most admire;
> They shut and open with a wire.'

Miss Dolly-girl told me she was much flatterated by the complimentation."

A knock at the door interrupted the conversation at this point, and on Boy's calling out "Come in," to their great surprise His Absolute Nothingness the Public Rhymester entered. He was weeping, and carried an

7

enormous pocket-handkerchief, which he put to his eyes every now and then.

"I heard that you were greatly in favour with the young Prince," he began, in a broken voice, "and thought I would ask you if you would kindly try and have me restored to my position as Court Poet again. I assure you I am not really half as bad as they tried to make out at the Committee Meeting this morning. The fact of the matter was I had just received a great shock, and it had driven all the poetry out of my head. Just as I was starting in the morning my wife told me that the cook had left and the man had called for the taxes. It was enough to upset any one, wasn't it?"

"Well," said Boy, who was a kind-hearted little fellow, "I don't know that we can do much for you, but I will certainly speak to the Prince on your behalf to-morrow if you wish."

"Oh, thank you! thank you very much, sir," said the Public Rhymester, brightening up at once, and vainly trying to stuff his handkerchief, which was quite as large as a small table-cloth, into his pocket. "And if I can ever do anything for you, write you a Valentine, you know, or your Epitaph, I shall be only too delighted."

One-and-Nine, who had been sitting bolt upright while

this conversation was going on, seemed to be suddenly struck with a bright inspiration.

"Are you an Oder?" he asked abruptly of the Public Rhymester.

"THE PUBLIC RHYMESTER ENTERED."

"An Oder?" repeated he vaguely. "What's that?"

"A person who writes Odes, of course," replied the Wooden Soldier; "because, if you are, I should be greatly obligated if you would kindly write one for me. I

intentionized writing it myself, but I have been con-
siderizing that it would be more properish to have it
written by a real Poet."

"Oh, thank you, sir, thank you!" cried the Public
Rhymester gratefully, "it is very kind indeed of you to
say that. A poor Poet, you know, gets very little praise
from any one nowadays, especially a Minor one, such as I
am. Why, a Grand Old Statesman said the other day
—but there, I mustn't let you into State Secrets. What
is the subject upon which you wish me to write?"

"Oh,—a—a—lady," said One-and-Nine bashfully, blushing up to the roots of his green paint.

"Of course," said the Public Rhymester smilingly; "it
usually is."

"And particularly about er—er—a—the corkscrew curls,
you know," said One-and-Nine, stammering nervously.
"Such delightfulish fascinationizing curls—six on each
side, you know—and they woggle when she shakes her
head—oh, dearest, *dearest* Martha Matilda," and the poor
Wooden Soldier seemed quite overcome by his emotions.

"Ah! these military men, these military men," said the
Public Rhymester, shaking his head, "what susceptible
creatures they are, to be sure, always in love with some
fair one or other! But there, we must do the best we

can for him, I suppose. What is the lady's name?" he inquired.

" Mrs. Martha Matilda Nimpky," replied One-and-Nine faintly.

" What! the Royal Nurse?" exclaimed the Public Rhymester in surprise.

The Wooden Soldier nodded his head.

" Well, I hope you'll win her," said the Public Rhymester, "though I think it's only fair to warn you that you must expect to have a great many rivals. Don't you see," he went on, " being Nurse to the little King, she is sure to have immense influence over him, and so will be one of the most important people in the kingdom. Oh, she's sure to have no end of suitors ; however, you are first in the field, and a handsome military man like yourself ought to stand a good chance. Now don't speak to me for a few moments while I write the poem for you.

The Wooden Soldier and Boy sat perfectly still while the Public Rhymester took a note-book and pencil from his pocket and began to walk rapidly up and down the apartment, pausing now and then to jot something down in his book, and occasionally clutching his hair and rolling his eyes about violently. Once Boy sneezed, and the Public Rhymester glared at him fiercely and then told him that he had entirely driven a beautiful word which *might* have rhymed with cucumber out of his head, and he would have to alter the whole verse. At last, however, the poem was finished and the Public Rhymester proudly read as follows :—

"TO MRS. M.   M.   N.
"Oh, Martha most majestic,
    Matilda quite sublime,
For thee I'd do the bravest deeds,
    Most giddy heights would climb.

"Oh! almond rock's delicious,
    And so is clotted cream,
And Birthday Cake is not so bad ;
    But these things tasteless seem ;

"For I have seen Matilda,
    And other joys have fled,
Her dazzling beauty's vanquished me,
    And turned my wooden head.

"I love thee, dear Matilda,
    Far more than other girls,
For there's not one amongst them all
    That wears such corkscrew curls.

"Such lovely little corkscrew curls,
    Just six on either side,
That woggle when you shake your head—
    Oh, will you be my bride?"

"Isn't the last line rather abrupteous?" inquired One-and-Nine when he had finished.

"Why, that's the best part about it," replied the Public Rhymester. "You see you pop the question so suddenly

"AFTER SAYING 'GOOD-NIGHT' TO BOY, RETIRED TO HIS OWN ROOM."

that you quite take the lady by storm—and that line comparing her to 'other girls' is very wise, you know; she is sure to feel flattered at that."

"Do you think that I ought to sign my name at the bottom of it?" asked One-and-Nine, folding the paper up neatly.

" I shouldn't if I were you," replied the Public Rhymester. " You can see what effect this has upon the lady, and if you think that she is pleased, I should follow it up with another, but I shouldn't sign my name at first ; it will make it a little mysterious, you know, and ladies like that sort of thing, I am told. But now I must be off. Good-night. You won't forget to do the best you can for me to-morrow, will you ? " and the Public Rhymester hurried away with his enormous handkerchief tucked under his arm, while One-and-Nine sealed up the Poem—after adding the follow-ing words, which he thought might improve it :

> " The rose is red, the violet's blue,
> Sardines are nice, and so are you "—

and handed it to Cæsar Maximilian Augustus Claudius Smith (called Thomas for short), to deliver, and then, after saying good-night to Boy, retired to his own room, which was on the other side of the corridor.

Boy sat up a little while longer, thinking of all the strange things which had been happening ; and then he followed the Wooden Soldier's example and went to rest too.

CHAPTER VII.

A STRANGE PARLIAMENT.

HEN Boy awoke the next morning he found the whole Palace in a commotion. Most of the Royal Household had been up all night making grand preparations for the Coronation of the young King. Out in the courtyard he could see the great gilded State Coach being dusted and brushed, while footmen and stewards were rushing about on all sorts of errands.

Boy heard from One-and-Nine that a carriage had been provided for them to join in the procession, which was to be a very extensive one. Animals were coming in of their own accord from all parts of the country to take part in it, and in the Park Boy was very much amused to see a worried-looking goose trying to teach a number of cocks and hens to march properly. The cocks were getting on famously, and held their heads up and stepped out bravely, but the hens would stop to peck at every worm and insect that they passed.

Several bands were practising in various parts of the grounds, and as they were all playing different tunes at the same time, the music was rather confusing.

Quite early in the morning the Lord High Adjudicator and most of the Court officials whom Boy had previously seen, arrived and began squabbling as to the order in which they should follow in the procession. The Advertiser General and the Public Rhymester were talking very excitedly about something or other. When the latter saw Boy he hurried up to him and said anxiously, " I hope you haven't spoken to the Prince about me yet ? "

" No," replied Boy, " I haven't seen him this morning."

" Ah, that's all right then," said the Public Rhymester, with a sigh of relief. " The Advertiser General has been explaining to me that I can earn ever so much more money as a Public Rhymester than a Court Poet, for you see I shall now be able to write poems for advertising purposes ; and he has already given me orders for several. I have to write a poem on ' Pea Soup for the Complexion,'

'Kofe's Hair Restorer for making the hair grow on worn-out brooms and brushes,' and a new Soap which 'won't wash clothes' or anything else—that's pretty good for a start, isn't it? So please don't say anything about my having the position of Court Poet restored to me, for I don't think that I would accept the post if it was offered me;" and the Public Rhymester went back to the Advertiser General again.

Boy could see that the carriages were beginning to form in a line, so he thought that it was time for him to get ready, and hurrying back to his apartments, found One-and-Nine waiting for him.

Soon after this the procession started, and before getting into the carriage with the Wooden Soldier Boy had a capital view of the young Prince as he entered the State Coach accompanied by the Royal Nurse. The dear little fellow looked very charming in a little white velvet suit with diamond buttons and buckles, and wore a plumed cap which he raised politely as the people cheered him along the route. Mrs. Martha Matilda Nimpky, too, looked very important in a yellow satin gown, with a bonnet trimmed with ribbons of all the colours of the rainbow.

Poor One-and-Nine was more lovesick than ever when

he beheld her, and scarcely noticed the beautiful decorations in the streets. Boy, however, was charmed with them. Flags and banners and triumphal arches were to be seen on all sides as they passed along, and Boy wondered how they could possibly have put them up in so short a time.

The Coronation ceremony itself was a very imposing one, and it was a beautiful sight to see the little King in his royal robes and crown and sceptre, whilst the people shouted most enthusiastically, "Long live the King, long live King Robert the Twenty-first" till they were hoarse. Then they had all gone with the Court dignitaries to the House of Words, where an address was read by the Lord High Adjudicator ; but by this time the poor little King was very tired indeed, and said that "he didn't want to hear all those old gentlemen talk any more."

Of course this was rather awkward, as there were several more State matters to be attended to, and the Royal Nurse tried to persuade the little King to stop and listen to them.

"These gentlemen, Your Majesty," said she, "are going to help you to be King and show you how to govern your subjects wisely ; you must hear what they have to say."

"But I don't want them," said His Majesty rebelliously, "I want some little boys to come to help me be King, not all these old gentlemans; and now I want to go back to the Palace and have my tea," and the little King got off the throne and toddled away with the Royal Nurse after him.

"Well, here's a pretty kettle of fish," said the Lord High Adjudicator when they had gone. "Of course as he is King he will have to be obeyed, but a parliament of children is positively absurd; and, besides, where shall we be? I can't think what's to be done."

"I suppose we couldn't dress up as children, could we?" suggested the Advertiser General after a pause.

"The very thing, of course," said the Lord High Adjudicator, delighted with this solution of the difficulty, and the meeting broke up in some disorder, after it had been arranged that they should all meet next morning attired as children and see if that would please the King.

In the evening there were fireworks and illuminations and a carnival in the streets, which people attended dressed in all sorts of fantastic garments.

Boy drove with One-and-Nine through the town to see the sights; everybody was provided with paper bags filled with "confetti" (which in this case were tiny little round pieces of coloured paper), with which they pelted each other. Boy quite enjoyed the fun, and tired himself out throwing confetti at the people as they passed, and getting handfuls thrown back at him, till the carriage was nearly filled with gaily coloured scraps of paper.

The King watched the sights from the Balcony of the Palace, and it was quite late before everybody got to bed and the town was quiet again.

At eleven o'clock the next morning the extraordinary Parliament met, and the King was already seated with the Royal Nurse beside him when the Politicians began to arrive. The Advertiser General looked very funny in a short baby's frock tied up with blue ribbons, while the Lord High Fiddle-de-dee, being rather tall, had adopted a sailor's suit, and trundled a hoop. The Lord High Adjudicator had overdone the matter and arrived in a perambulator accompanied by a nurse carrying a feeding-bottle. All the others were dressed as children too, and most of them carried toys, and the noise of the penny trumpets which many of them blew was quite deafening. (*See* FRONTISPIECE).

The little King laughed when he saw them, and declared that it was great fun and much better than such a lot of talking about things that he couldn't understand.

He ordered that all the seats should be taken out of the hall so that they could play games and use the toys which the Statesmen had brought ; he had, moreover, insisted on the Lord High Fiddle-de-dee going down on

"TIRED HIMSELF OUT THROWING CONFETTI AT THE PEOPLE.

his hands and knees and giving him a ride on his back all round the room. Then they had gone out on to the Terrace which was outside the House of Words and by which the river ran, and the King had screamed with delight when, at Boy's suggestion, all the old gentlemen played at leapfrog, doing their best to look dignified in these trying circumstances; then when they were all tired out, they went back to the hall again and sat in a ring on the floor looking quite exhausted, while the King demanded Nursery Rhymes.

The Busybody Extraordinary, who had been exerting himself more than all the others in his efforts to please the King, immediately commenced to repeat the following :—

> "Sing a song of sixpence,
>   A pocket full of Rye,
>   About a foolish serving maid,
>   To tell you I will try.

> "The King was in his counting-house
>   Bemoaning lack of money,
>   The Knave was in the pantry
>   Stealing bread and honey.

> "The Queen was in her tiring-room
>   Just trying a new dress,
>   'The last one isn't paid for yet,'
>   I heard the Queen confess.

> "The maid was in the garden
>   Hanging out the clothes,
>   While four-and-twenty dicky birds
>   She balanced on her nose.

"'FOUR-AND-TWENTY DICKY BIRDS SHE BALANCED ON HER NOSE.'"

8

"And while the birdies sat there,
This maid began to sing.
'I say, you know, I can't stand that,'
Called out the angry King.

"The maid she sang so out of tune
It nearly drove him mad,
So the Chamberlain discharged her,
And every one was glad."

"Aren't you going to repeat the moral?" asked the Lord High Fiddle-de-dee when he had finished.

"There isn't one," said the Busybody Extraordinary.

"Yes, there is ; in fact, there are four morals to it," said the Lord High Fiddle-de-dee. "Aren't there?" he asked, appealing to the others, who nodded.

"What are they then?" said the Busybody Extraordinary.

"Don't always wear your Sunday clothes,
Or it will make you vain.

That's one," replied the Advertiser General.

"Don't balance birds upon your nose,
Or you'll be thought insane.

That's another," said the Lord High Fiddle-de-dee.

"If any one sings out of tune,
It's not much use to scold.

That's the third," chimed in the First Lord of the Cash
Box.

> " And if your voice is very harsh,
> Don't sing unless you're told.

And that's the fourth," added the Lord High Adjudicator.

" More," shouted the King, clapping his hands, and the
Kitchen Poker in Waiting got up and said,—

" I know a short one, Your Majesty."

" Go on," replied the little King.

> " Hey diddle diddle the cat couldn't fiddle,
> The cow turned her back on the moon,
> The little dog said, ' This is very poor sport,'
> And the dish had a row with the spoon,"

repeated the Kitchen Poker in Waiting.

" Is that all? " asked the King. " Doesn't any one else
know another ? "

" I think," said Boy, "that I could repeat ' Simple
Simon.' "

" That's right," cried His Majesty ; "try."

So Boy began :

> " Simple Simon went a-skating
> On a pond in June.
> ' Dear me,' he cried, ' this water's wet,
> I fear I've come too soon.'

" Simple Simon saw a sparrow
    Flying through the air.
' Why shouldn't I have wings ? ' he cried ;
    ' I'm sure it isn't fair.'

" So simple Simon bought some feathers,
    Made a pair of wings ;
And now he's broken both his legs
    He calls them ' foolish things.'

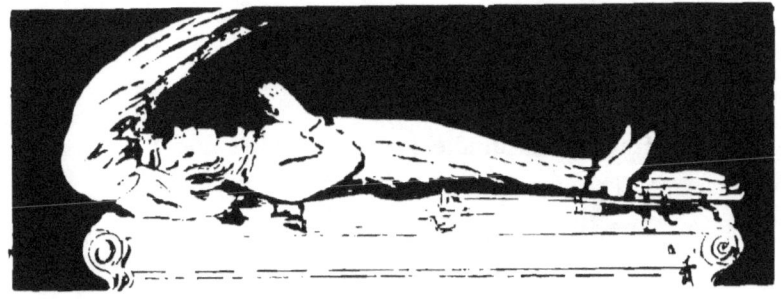

" ' HE HELD THE GUN THE WRONG WAY ROUND, AND SHOT HIMSELF
INSTEAD.' "

" Simple Simon bought a gun,
    ' To shoot some game,' he said.
He held the gun the wrong way round,
    And shot himself instead."

His Majesty seemed very pleased with this rhyme,
and Boy had to say it over again. Then the King
proposed a game of blind man's buff, and they had a
fine time in the old Hall, till tea was ready, when they
all went out on to the Terrace again and had it served

at little tables. They had the bread and jam cut rather thick because they were all very hungry after their exertions, and as His Majesty drank milk and water, the others were obliged to do the same. Boy could see the Lord High Adjudicator and the Lord High Fiddle-de-dee making very wry faces over it; but it would not have been considered etiquette for them to have tea while the King drank milk and water.

Soon after tea His Majesty went back to the Palace after telling them all that he had enjoyed himself very much indeed and hoped to see them all the next day.

"That's all very well," said the Lord High Adjudicator, when His Majesty and the Royal Nurse had gone, "but I don't see how the Public affairs can be attended to while this sort of thing goes on. I can quite see that having a King so young as His Majesty may cause us considerable difficulty in the future."

"That is very easily remedied, gentlemen," said a voice from the other end of the Hall, and turning around they beheld an extraordinary-looking old man, in a long, flowing red gown and a high conical hat. His beard, which was very long, was perfectly white, while bushy black eyebrows shaded a pair of very bright, piercing eyes; his hat and gown were both embroidered with

a number of mysterious-looking figures and signs. How
he had entered the Hall was a mystery, for no one
saw him come in, and there was no door near where he
was standing.

"That's very easily remedied, gentlemen," he repeated,
glancing rapidly from one to the other from under his
shaggy eyebrows. "I can very soon help you out of
the difficulty if you wish, for I am 'Ohah,' the Magician.
You may have heard of me before."

CHAPTER VIII.

OHAH, THE MAGICIAN.

HE greatest consternation followed this announcement, and the Lord High Adjudicator in particular looked greatly alarmed.

"Wh—wh—what do you want?" he stammered nervously.

"I think I have the pleasure of addressing His Importance the Lord High Adjudicator, have I not?" replied Ohah. "I scarcely recognised you in that—ahem--that costume," he added, smiling sarcastically.

"Oh, I wear it for the sake of coolness," said the Lord High Adjudicator, hastily rearranging his bib, which was somewhat disordered. "We have been having very warm weather lately, you know."

'Oh! really!" said Ohah. "And I suppose you play leapfrog and blind man's buff for the sake of coolness too, eh? I should have thought that at your time of life you had given up such frivolities."

"It was His Majesty's fault," said the Lord High Adjudicator sheepishly; "he *would* have a parliament of children, and so we were obliged to dress like this and play games, or we should have lost our positions."

"H'm! doesn't it strike you as being rather foolish to have a King so young as your present one?" inquired Ohah.

"Well, it certainly has its disadvantages," admitted the Lord High Adjudicator; "but what are we to do? He is the lawful successor to the throne, you know."

"Well, I could soon help you out of that difficulty if you wished," said the Magician, a cunning look creeping over his face.

"What do you mean?" asked the Lord High Adjudicator.

"I could make him invisible, you know, like the Prince and Princess, and then you could govern the country yourselves," suggested Ohah.

"Oh, but that wouldn't be right, surely," said the Lord High Adjudicator.

"Oh, I don't know," chimed in the Busybody Extraordinary; "we sha'n't be able to manage very well with a King like this, and if there was no legal successor to the throne we could have a general election, you know, and choose a King for ourselves."

"Does it hurt much to be made invisible?" asked the Lord High Adjudicator thoughtfully.

"Not a bit," exclaimed Ohah; "it's rather a pleasant sensation than otherwise."

"And how long would he have to remain in that state?" inquired the Lord High Adjudicator.

"Oh! till the Portmanteau is found," was the reply.

"The Portmanteau!" exclaimed the Lord High Adjudicator; "why, that will never be found, you know; we had every house in Zum searched for it years ago."

"It must be here somewhere, and when it is found I am instructed by the King of Limesia to make your Crown Prince and his bride visible again; but in the meantime you had better let me make the little King invisible too, for you can't possibly go on as you are."

"What do you think about it?" asked the Lord High Adjudicator of the others.

"Well, I don't think it's at all a bad plan, do you know," replied the Advertiser General. "I can see that we shall have rather a hard time of it if His present Majesty continues to reign; and if it wouldn't hurt him at all——"

"Not in the least," interrupted Ohah.

"I don't see why we shouldn't agree to it."

"That's right! and now, when shall I perform the operation?" said Ohah in a business-like way.

"Oh, the sooner the quicker," replied the Advertiser General. "What do you say to to-morrow morning?"

"Yes, that will suit me nicely," was the answer; and so it was arranged that the poor little King should be rendered invisible the next day; but Boy, who had been listening eagerly to all that had been going on, made up his mind that he would do what he could to prevent it, so calling One-and-Nine, he hurried to the Palace, and sent a message to the Royal Nurse to say that he must have an interview with her immediately.

Mrs. Martha Matilda Nimpky received him in her own apartments, and listened intently to all that he had to say.

"The wretches!" she exclaimed. "And that old villain Ohah! Of course he has been sent by that horrible King of Limesia; who directly he has got rid of this poor little fellow will come here and seize the throne for himself: I can see through his little tricks and manners."

"But what's to be done?" cried Boy excitedly. "We must do something to prevent it. I know," he exclaimed after thinking for a moment, "Professor Crab, of course. You could go and stay at his house with His Majesty till we could find another place for him. Ohah wouldn't think of looking there, I am sure."

"Where is Professor Crab's?" inquired the Royal Nurse.

"Drinkon College," replied Boy. "You go by the Submarine Navigation Company's Steamers, you know, and I will get One-and-Nine to escort you to the College, while I stop here and see what goes on in your absence."

"Do you mean that Soldier friend of yours?" inquired Mrs. Martha Matilda Nimpky, blushing bashfully. "He seems to be a very nice gentleman."

"Yes, he is," replied Boy, "and he will be delighted, I am sure, to act as your escort, for he admires you very much indeed."

"Does he really?" said Mrs. Martha Matilda Nimpky, giggling and shaking her curls coquettishly. "How nice!"

"I don't think there's any time to lose," said Boy;

"you go and prepare His Majesty, and I will go with you to the Station."

A very few moments later they all met in the garden, and after Boy had formally introduced One-and-Nine to Mrs. Martha Matilda Nimpky, they left the Palace grounds by a small private gate, and after one or two inquiries found themselves at the Quay. Fortunately there was a boat starting soon, and so they were off, and Boy was back again to the Palace before any one had missed them. He had barely, however, reached his apartments in the Palace when Cæsar Maximilian Augustus Claudius Smith (called Thomas for short) brought him a card on which Boy read :

PROFESSOR OHAH.

COURT MAGICIAN TO HIS MAJESTY THE KING OF LIMESIA.

Necromancy.   Astrology.
Legerdemain.   Hocus Pocus,
and Sleight of Hand.

———

Objectionable relatives removed on the shortest notice.
Umbrellas recovered while you wait.

" Dear me, I wonder what he wants to see me for?" he thought as he waited for the Magician to enter.

" I thought you'd like to see some tricks," said this gentleman as he came in, "and it will be good practice for me for my important work to-morrow. Now is there anything that you'd like to be turned into?"

"Oh no, thank you," cried Boy, greatly alarmed, "I'm quite content to be myself."

"H'm! you are an exception to the general rule then. However, you *must* be changed to something or other, for I want to have some practice. What do you say to being a hen?" and the Magician stretched out his hands and made a few mysterious passes, muttering some strange words the while.

Boy was just going to cry, "Oh! please no," when he found to his great dismay that he could not speak, and the only noise which he could make sounded like "tuk-tuk-tuk-tuk ka-r-a-a-ka, tuk-tuk-tuk-tuk ka-ra-a-ka," and when he looked down at his feet he found claws there instead, and feathers on his body; in fact, he was completely transformed. He tried to scream, but "tuk-tuk-tuk-tuk-tuk-ka-r-a-a-ka" was the result, and Ohah was holding his sides with laughter while Boy ran and flew frantically about the room, making this strange noise and clumsily knocking his beak against the furniture on all sides, till presently he managed to get under a chair at the further end of the room and miserably wondered what would happen next.

Cæsar Maximilian Augustus Claudius Smith (called

"TUK-TUK-TUK-TUK KA-R-A-A-KA."

Thomas for short) hearing the noise rushed into the room, and made matters worse by trying to drive the poor bewildered hen out.

"Shoo-shoo," he cried, kicking under the chair, and Boy flew out again and ran round and round the room calling out "tuk-tuk-tuk-tuk-ka-ra-a-ka," "tuk-tuk-tuk-tuk ka-ra-a-a-ka" as loudly as he could till presently Ohah (who had been laughing the whole time) made some further passes with his hand and muttered some more words, and Cæsar Maximilian Augustus Claudius Smith (called Thomas for short) changed at once into a little dog.

"Bow-wow-wow, yap-yap," he barked, rushing at Boy; and then the old chase began all over again, till at last by a great effort Boy flew up on to the bookcase out of his reach. He felt very hot and tired, and forgetting that he was a hen, began fumbling about for his handkerchief, and in doing so nearly lost his balance and fell off his uncomfortable perch. He felt greatly relieved when Ohah transformed Cæsar Maximilian Augustus Claudius Smith (called Thomas for short) back to himself again, and as soon as he had done so Boy flew down on to the floor; and it was as well that he did, for with a wave of his wand (which he carried up his sleeve) the Magician just then turned the bookcase into a big humming-top and afterwards into a pair of steps, and then, apparently satisfied that his powers as a Magician were in good working order, he suddenly restored Boy and the bookcase to their original forms again.

"Oh," cried Boy with a sigh of relief when he found that he was himself once more, "that's very interesting, sir, but please don't do it again."

"Why not?" laughed Ohah. "It's as simple as A.B.C.; there is no danger."

"Can you change yourself into things too?" inquired Boy.

"Yes!" said Ohah. "Would you like to see me? What shall I be?"

"Oh, something small, please. I should be terribly frightened if you were to turn into a lion or bear, you see."

"All right," said Ohah, "I'll be a Kottle."

"What's that?" cried Boy.

"Oh, a thing all *gribbins* and *bones*," explained Ohah. "Now watch," and he waved his wand about his head two or three times, and then disappeared.

Boy watched intently, for he wanted very much to find out what a Kottle was; nothing appeared, though, except one or two oddly-shaped scraps of paper, which Boy picked up and tried to fit together, for there was something written on the back of them; at last he was able to make out the following words :—"*I have forgotten how to change myself back from a Kottle again. Good-bye for ever, Ohah.*"

"There!" exclaimed Boy. "Well, I must say I'm not very sorry, for he must have been a most dangerous

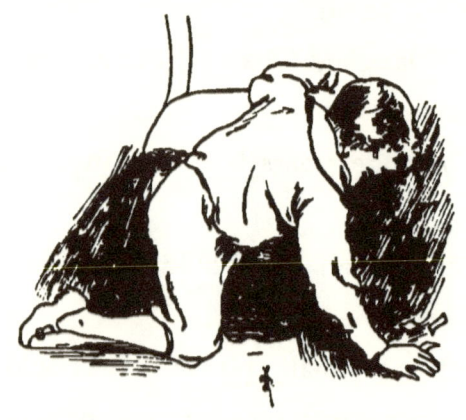

"ONE OR TWO ODDLY-SHAPED SCRAPS OF PAPER."

person to have about. I *should* have liked to have found out what a Kottle was, though."

But he never did, and I may mention here that at Zum to this day they have a habit of saying about anything that they don't understand, "Oh, it must be a Kottle."

When Boy found that there was no chance of Ohah reappearing, he wondered if he ought to send for the

young King and the Royal Nurse to come back again,
but finally decided that in the present unsettled state of
public opinion it would be safer to wait a little while
and see what happened ; because if the Lord High Adjudicator and the other Statesmen were treacherous
enough to hand the little King over to the tender mercies
of Ohah, Boy felt that he was not at all safe in their
hands.

Shortly after this it was discovered that the King and
the Royal Nurse were missing, and the Lord High Adjudicator and the others flocked to the Palace to find
out if it were true.

Cæsar Maximilian Augustus Claudius Smith (called
Thomas for short) explained what had happened to
himself ; and it was at once decided that Ohah must have
made the little King invisible rather sooner than he had
intended, and they all went back to the House of Words
to talk over the situation.

"Of course we must have a general election at once,"
said the Lord High Adjudicator when they had all
settled down into their places, "to decide who is to be
made King."

"I am still willing to accept the post, if you like,"
suggested the Kitchen Poker in Waiting disinterestedly.

"It will save the trouble of an election, you know; and I don't wish to boast, but I am quite sure that you could not possibly select anybody nearly so suitable for the position as myself. Handsome, accomplished and modest to a degree, I——"

"Here, here, that's quite enough of that," interrupted the Advertiser General. "We have decided to elect a King by vote, and there's an end of the matter. I will go and have some posters printed and stuck about all over the town, and we'll soon have this matter put right. I shouldn't be at all surprised if I were elected myself. I'm a very popular man, you know."

"H'm!" sneered the Lord High Adjudicator, "I don't think you will stand much chance if I put up for the post, as I certainly intend to do."

"Well, don't let's waste time wrangling," suggested the Busybody Extraordinary; "let's decide when the election is to take place."

"Oh, to-morrow, of course," was the cry; "the sooner the better."

So a notice was drawn up as follows, and the Advertiser General was instructed to have it printed and posted on all the walls some time that night, however late it might be.

NOTICE!

---◆---

Whereas His Majesty, King Robert the Twenty-first, has mysteriously disappeared and there is no successor to the throne, an

ELECTION

OF A

SUITABLE KING

will take place to-morrow at the House of Words. Each person to have one vote. Polling papers can be had of the Town Clerk and must be filled up and returned by two o'clock in the afternoon, when the Poll will be closed.

By Order,

JOSHUA DOBBS,

Lord High Adjudicator.

And as soon as this business was concluded the meeting broke up, and every one hurried away to try and secure votes for himself.

The news spread like wild fire, and as he went back to the Palace, Boy could see excited groups of people, and

even animals, discussing the matter, and on opening his
window when he reached his apartments he disturbed

"VOTE FOR MR. THOMAS CAT."

a large black cat who had just finished writing a placard
on which Boy could discern the words :—

VOTE

FOR

MR. THOMAS CAT,

A SICK WIFE AND SEVEN SMALL KITTENS.

Boy shut the window and went to bed.

CHAPTER IX.

THE ELECTION.

OY was awakened very early the next morning by Cæsar Maximilian Augustus Claudius Smith (called Thomas for short), who remarked with a haughty air while setting the breakfast things,—

"I don't suppose you will have me to wait upon you to-morrow morning, sir."

"Why not?" inquired Boy.

"I shall very likely have been made King by that time," remarked the footman with his nose in the air. "You can still stay at the Palace, though, if you like."

"Really!" exclaimed Boy. "Have you been elected then?" he asked, forgetting that the Election did not take place till two o'clock in the afternoon.

"Not yet," admitted the footman, "but I'm pretty sure to be, because of my name, you know."

"Smith?" inquired Boy.

"No, the others," said the footman impatiently. "Cæsar was a king, I've heard, and so was Augustus, so was Maximilian, and so was Claudius, I believe."

"No, they were all emperors," corrected Boy. "Cæsar, Augustus, and Claudius, were emperors of Rome, and Maximilian was Emperor of Germany. We heard all about them in our History class last term."

"Are you sure, sir?" asked the footman mournfully.

"Yes, quite!" replied Boy decidedly.

"Dear me," cried the poor man, "I'm afraid that I don't stand quite as much chance as I thought I did. What a pity! I've ordered my crown and things, too," he continued. "Never mind! perhaps I may be elected after all. I suppose, sir, if I offered to vote for you, you wouldn't vote for me, would you?"

"I don't see how that would be of much use," exclaimed Boy.

"Well, every vote helps, you know," said Cæsar Maximilian Augustus Claudius Smith (called Thomas for short). "Shall I go and get the polling papers?"

Boy thought that it couldn't possibly do much harm,

so just to please him he told the footman that he might go and get them ; and when he returned a few minutes later they were both solemnly filled up and taken back to the Ballot Box.   Then Boy finished his breakfast and started for a walk.

The streets were filled with excited groups of people discussing their own prospects of being elected King, and the walls were covered with posters of all shapes and sizes begging for votes.   One enterprising man was offering *a thousand pounds* to every one who would vote for him.

" Why, however can he pay them all ? " exclaimed Boy to a person in the street.

" Oh ! people are never expected to keep the promises made at elections," explained the man.   " Now I don't promise anything at all, but you only just vote for me and see what *I'll* do for you if I'm made King."

" I can't," said Boy.   " I've already voted."

" Oh, bother ! " cried the man, " you're no good to me, then," and he hurried on to the next person and began to beg for his vote.

Boy was soon surrounded by people bothering him to vote for them and was quite glad to escape down a by-street where there was scarcely any one to be seen, and where his attention was attracted by a curious-looking sign affixed to a house worded like this.—

ƎHⱢ ⱯƎSIⱢⱤƎΛꓷⱯ ⅂ⱯⱤƎNƎ⅁ SIHⱢ ΛⱯM NI

"What a funny sign!" thought Boy. "I wonder what it means?" and he was still wondering when a Butcher's Bill passed. He was a very tall boy and carried a butcher's tray on his shoulder. Of course, he was whistling —all butcher boys do—but he stopped when he saw Boy and came up to where he was standing.

"Can you tell me what that means, please?" asked Boy, pointing to the sign.

"Can't you read?" asked the Butcher's Bill.

"Not Greek," replied Boy. "That is Greek, isn't it?" he asked; for it looked to him very much like an inscription that he had once seen carved over a big building in London, and which his Uncle had told him was Greek.

"Greek! your grandmother!" exclaimed the Butcher's Bill rudely. "It's Upside Downish."

"What's that?" asked Boy.

"I'll tell you if you promise me your vote," said the Butcher's Bill.

"I'm very sorry," replied Boy, "but I've already given it."

"Then stand on your head and find out for yourself," cried the rude Butcher's Bill, shouldering his tray and walking off again whistling loudly.

"I wonder what he means?" thought Boy, staring at the letters; he could make nothing of them, though, and was just going to walk away when he saw the Advertiser General looking out of one of the windows above the signboard.

"Come in," he called. "I want to speak to you very particularly."

Boy pushed the door open and found some steps inside which led up to a large studio, in which he found the Advertiser General and the Public Rhymester.

They both rushed at him as soon as he entered the door and each seized one of his arms.

"Please promise me your vote," they both exclaimed in one breath.

"Oh dear!" cried Boy, "I'm quite tired of telling everybody I have already voted."

The Advertiser General and the Public Rhymester both looked greatly disappointed, and each let go of his arm and went back to his work.

"What are you doing, please?" inquired Boy.

"Can't you see?" replied the Advertiser General snappishly. "We're making advertisements. Have you finished that Poem for Watzematta Tea yet?" he asked of the Public Rhymester.

"Very nearly," he replied with some confusion, hastily screwing up some paper which he held in his hands into a ball.

"What's that?" demanded the Advertiser General; "let me see."

The Public Rhymester handed him the ball of paper, which the Advertiser General carefully smoothed out.

"Did any one ever see such rubbish?" he exclaimed after he had read it. "Why, you've mixed yourself up so with the tea that one can't tell which is which. Just read this," and he handed Boy the crumpled pieces of paper, on which were written the following words:

"Delicious Watzematta is a very soothing tea,
And when you're voting for a King, oh, please remember me.
It's cheaper far than other sorts; it's flavour's full and free—
And that I'd make a charming King, I'm sure you'll all agree.

"One cup of Watzematta will equal any three
Of other kinds; it is so nice—and so am I, you see.
There never was another King so good as I will be.
Pour boiling water on it (the tea I mean, not me)."

" Well, it certainly is rather mixed," said Boy when he
had finished reading this curious advertisement.

" Oh ! I can't settle down to anything till this Election
is over," complained the Public Rhymester. " How are
you getting on ? " he asked, walking over to where the
Advertiser General was painting an enormous poster.
" Why, you are as bad as I am," he cried. " Look at
that ! " and he pointed to a part of the poster on which
the Advertiser General had painted the words :

**" Use Bluntpoint's Needles. To be had of all
respectable kings."**

" Good gracious, I meant drapers, of course," cried the
Advertiser General, throwing down his brush. " Well,
it's evidently no use trying to work till after the
Election ; we are all far too excited."

" I was going to ask you," said Boy, " what those words
outside this house meant."

" Oh ! " said the Advertiser General, " that is a very
ingenious advertisement of mine. You see the words are
simply turned upside down, so you have to stand on your
head to read them properly. It's a capital idea. You
see the great thing in advertising is to impress the advertisement on the public mind, and if one has to stand
on his head the whole of the time he is reading it

through, he is not likely to forget it in a hurry, is he?
This was the first advertisement ever written in that

"'THIS WAS THE FIRST ADVERTISEMENT EVER WRITTEN IN THAT WAY.'"

way," and the Advertiser General brought from a portfolio
a large card bearing these words:

KING'S PORTMANTEAU?
GOOD-MORNING, HAVE YOU SEEN THE

"What *is* all this nonsense about the Portmanteau?"
exclaimed Boy. "I'm always hearing something or other
about it. Whose was it?"

"Ah! it may seem nonsense to you, but I assure you it was a very serious matter for us at the time," said the Advertiser General, while the Public Rhymester nodded his head emphatically.

"You see the King of Limesia and our late sovereign King Robert the Twentieth were very great friends, and the King of Limesia came to Zum on a visit. Oh, it was a grand time, I can tell you. The streets were decorated, and there were speeches and processions, and he was presented with the freedom of the city in a casket made of solid gingerbread gilded over so that it looked like real gold, and which he could eat when he got tired of looking at."

"I think that's a very good idea," interrupted Boy. "I have often read of people being presented with addresses and things in gold caskets, and I always wondered whatever use they could possibly be to them afterwards."

"Well," continued the Advertiser General, "things went on swimmingly for a few days till suddenly the King of Limesia's Portmanteau disappeared very mysteriously. No one had the slightest idea when, where, or how. You would never believe the commotion it caused. Both Kings were furious. King Robert declared that it *must* and *should* be found, and had an organised search made

"'THE STREETS FULL OF PEOPLE ALL STANDING ON THEIR HEADS.'"

in every house in Zum. Not one was passed without having every room ransacked. The King of Limesia declared that he would not remain a single day longer, and went off in a huff, and altogether there was such a set out as you never saw."

"What was there in the Portmanteau?" asked Boy.

"Why, all the King's clean collars, a new toothbrush, a receipt for making toffee and lots of things. Well, I had to prepare a special Poster to be stuck about the town, and by a splendid piece of good fortune I thought of this system of advertising. It was great success and caused an enormous sensation. Just fancy seeing the streets full of people all standing on their heads at the same time reading the advertisement. The King was delighted and made sure that we should soon find the Portmanteau. We never did, though, to this day," said the Advertiser General mournfully, "and the King of Limesia and our late King never made up the quarrel about it."

"Well," said Boy, I think it was rather silly to make all that fuss about an old Portm———"

But before he could finish the sentence cries of "Haste to the poll," "Haste to the poll" were heard in the street, and on looking out of the window they saw people rushing frantically towards the House of Words. Hastily snatching up their caps the Advertiser General and the Public Rhymester rushed down the stairs and out into the road, and were soon lost to sight in the crowd. Boy followed as quickly as he could, for he wanted to hear who had been elected King. He could not get near the House of Words because of the crowd, but he could see by a clock in the street that it was nearly two, so the suspense would soon be over.

"Do you think that I stand any chance, sir?" inquired a melancholy-looking person standing near Boy.

"I'm sure I don't know," replied he.

"Because if I do I don't know however I shall be able to afford a crown and sceptre. Are they very expensive, do you know?"

"Why, I should think they would be provided for you if you were elected King, wouldn't they?" asked Boy.

"I'm sure I don't know. I wish I hadn't gone in for it at all," replied the man; "I'm a shoemaker by trade, and my wife she said to me, 'What a fine thing it would be if you were elected King!' so I voted for myself. I am rather sorry I did so now, because I don't know anything about reigning, and I'm afraid I sha'n't make a very good King if I am elected."

Before Boy could reply there was a great shout, and

two o'clock struck from the clock tower above the House of Words.

"Now we shall soon know," said Boy; and sure enough

"'HIS MAJESTY HAD GIVEN UP BUSINESS.'"

in a few moments the Lord High Adjudicator came to the top of the steps, and with a very white face announced that everybody had the same number of votes, so that they were *all* elected Kings; and it turned out afterwards that everybody but Boy and Cæsar Maximilian Augustus

Claudius Smith (called Thomas for short) had voted for themselves, and as those two had voted for each other it came to the same thing.

It was very comical to see the airs the people at once began to give themselves when they realised what had happened, and even the poor Shoemaker King stared in a haughty way at Boy, and did not deign even to say good-day as he hurried home to tell his wife the news.

Boy was heartily amused, and the more so when he heard the very Butcher's Bill that he had seen in the morning say to another Bill of about the same age as himself,—

"Look here, Your Majesty, if I have any more of Your Majesty's cheek I shall have to punch Your Majesty's royal nose, and if Your Majesty wishes to fight, come on."

To which the other boy, who had previously been a Grocer's Bill, replied,—

"Your Majesty may be a King, but you are no gentleman, and I would not bemean myself by condescending to fight with Your Majesty;" and with a scornful look the late Grocer's Bill passed on.

"Well, I expect there will be a pretty muddle presently if all these people are to be Kings," thought Boy, quite forgetting that he was a King himself under these circumstances ; and it was not until he had tried to buy a penny bun, and had been told by the baker's wife that "His Majesty had given up business," that he realised how very awkward it might become.

CHAPTER X.

URRYING back to the Palace Boy found a great crowd of people on the steps at the principal entrance—most of them carried bundles and parcels, and some even had articles of furniture on their heads.

"Why, whatever is happening now ? " he thought, and on inquiry he found that these were some of the newly elected Kings coming to take possession of the Palace.

King Cæsar Maximilian Augustus Claudius Smith (now called King Smith I.), whose crown had not yet arrived, had ingeniously contrived a temporary one of alternate silver forks and spoons stuck in the band of his hat, and, with a velvet pile table-cloth from one of the drawing-room tables thrown over his shoulder,

152

looked quite imposing as he stood at the door and explained to the people that he was now as much a King as the rest of them, and intended to keep the Palace for himself.

" *You* may come in, though," he said, catching sight of Boy, and as soon as he had entered, King Smith I. closed and bolted the door, and the other disappointed Kings had to carry their bundles and parcels home again.

" How do you like being a King, Your Majesty ? " asked King Smith I. pleasantly, when they had reached one of the state apartments in which he had established himself.

" Well, I don't know," laughed Boy, " I don't feel any different at present."

" Ah ! that's because you haven't a crown and sceptre, Your Majesty ; we must see what we can find for you. You are sure to be treated with disrespect if you don't main-tain your kingly dignity. The late Lord High Adjudicator, who is now King Joshua Dobbs, seized the regalia as soon as he knew that he was elected King, and so the rest of us will have to make shift with such crowns and things as we can manufacture for ourselves. Now let's see. What can we make you a crown out of? Oh ! I know. There are some packets of tea downstairs with some beautiful silver paper around them ; suppose we make you a crown of that, and twist some around a stick for a sceptre."

So with some paste and cardboard and this silver paper, which King Smith I. brought up from downstairs, they soon made quite a respectable-looking crown, and particularly as King Smith I. had found some fancy buttons, which he fastened into it, to look like jewels. Another small table-cloth, pinned to Boy's shoulders for a cloak, completed his costume, and he felt quite proud of his appearance when he saw his reflection in the looking-glass at the end of the room.

"Will there be any meeting in the House of Words to-day ? " asked Boy, " and if so who will sit on the Throne ? I expect there will be a rare scramble for it, won't there ? "

King Smith I. laughed.

" The Busybody Extraordinary," he said, " took possession of it immediately he heard that he had been elected King and won't leave it on any consideration whatever. He has sat in it ever since the Election and at first declared that he would carry it about with him wherever he went, and when he found that it was too heavy to move, he sent for his wife and family, and they have taken up their residence on the dais on which it is placed, and intend to remain there. The First Lord of the Cash Box has the best of it, though, for he has all the money—he absolutely refuses to part with a penny ;

" HE FELT QUITE PROUD OF HIS APPEARANCE.'

and although I tried to persuade him that I ought to have an allowance made me as I was now a King, he wouldn't see it. He said that if he made every one who was elected an allowance he would have no money left for himself."

"What time do we dine to-day?" asked Boy, who began to feel rather hungry.

"Well, you see," explained King Smith, "all the other servants have left, and I expect we shall have to manage for ourselves; fortunately there is plenty of food in the larder, but who's to set the table? I don't think, now that I am a King, I ought to have to do that sort of thing, you know."

"Oh! I don't mind helping to set the table," suggested Boy, if you will show me where the things are."

"Very well, Your Majesty," said King Smith I.; "one King is as good as another, and if you don't mind helping we will soon have a nice little dinner party all to ourselves."

So Boy and he went down into the great empty kitchens, and brought up plates and dishes and laid them in great state in the Banqueting Hall, and with the pies and pasties which they found in the pantry they had quite a feast.

After they had enjoyed their dinner, King Smith I. washed the dishes, and Boy wiped them and put them away, and then he thought that he would like to stroll into the town and see what was going on. He found the streets full of Kings and Queens dressed with the

"THEY ALL SEEMED PRETTY WELL SATISFIED WITH THEMSELVES."

most ridiculous attempts at royal grandeur ; the Queens wore long court trains made of table-cloths and window-curtains, and any other old finery that they could scrape together at such short notice, while the Kings did their best to appear grand with such odds and ends as were left.

Dish-covers and fireirons were very fashionable substitutes for crowns and sceptres, which, of course, were necessary for everybody.

Boy's crown of tinsel paper was evidently much admired, and many of the Kings and Queens cast envious glances at it as he walked through the streets. On the whole, though, they all seemed pretty well satisfied with themselves, and treated each other with a considerable amount of hauteur.

Boy called in at the House of Words just out of curiosity to see the Busybody Extraordinary, and found him, looking very dignified indeed, seated on the great gilded throne at one end of the Hall ; the effect was rather marred, though, by the dais being littered with all kinds of household furniture which had been hastily brought across from his old home. Her Majesty the Queen, his wife, was busy making up a bed for the baby on one of the lower steps, and the Princess, his daughter, and the Crown Prince, his son, were squabbling as to who should wash up the dinner plates in a tin pail at the back of the throne.

They received Boy in great state, however, for when they perceived him coming towards them the King arose and the Queen and the Prince and Princess formed a group around him, with their noses in the air in a very superior style, and the Queen informed Boy that "he might kiss her hand if he wished."

Boy, however, said, "it didn't matter, thank you, and he had only called to see how they liked living on the dais."

"Oh, of course," said the King with a grand air, "it's only for a very short time—until I have an opportunity of re-organising my Kingdom. It's rather awkward, at present, you see, there being so many other Kings and Queens about."

"Yes, I should think so," laughed Boy.

The King got down from the throne, and coming close to Boy, whispered in his ear,—

"Would you mind calling me 'Your Majesty' when you speak to me, please?" and then went back to his throne again.

"What nonsense!" replied Boy. "I can't keep

addressing everybody as 'Your Majesty,' you know, and, besides, I'm as much of a King as you are."

The Queen looked very severe.

" What shall we do about it, my dear ? " asked the King anxiously.

" AS TO WHO SHOULD WASH UP THE DINNER PLATES IN A TIN PAIL
AT THE BACK OF THE THRONE."

" Send him to the deepest dungeon beneath the Castle Moat," replied the Queen, waving her hand tragically.

" Yes, we shall really have to do something of that sort, if you don't treat us with proper respect," remarked the King warningly.

" What rubbish ! " laughed Boy. " Why, you haven't got a castle moat, or a dungeon either," and he walked away while the King sat down on the throne with a great air of offended dignity, and the rest of the Royal family resumed their domestic duties.

Out in the town Boy found all the shops closed ; for, you see, none of the Kings and Queens would think of working, and so everything was at a standstill.

After hunting about for a little time Boy found the house where the Advertiser General had lived, and thought he would call on him. He found him seated at one end of the long studio while the Public Rhymester sat at the other ; they had each arranged a chair on the top of a table to look something like a throne, and the Advertiser General had really made a very regal-looking cloak out of a large piece of calico, by painting one side red and drawing little black tails on the other to look like ermine. They seemed very miserable, though, and explained to Boy that they had not been able to get anything to eat.

"We went out a little while ago," complained the Advertiser General, "but His Majesty the butcher was most rude when I commanded him to send me some meat for dinner, and Her Majesty his wife asked me 'if I knew who I was talking to?'

"It was just the same with His Majesty the grocer. He was seated in state on a sugar-barrel at one end of his shop, which he now calls the Palace, and would no more think of serving me with a pound of tea than if he had been the Emperor of China himself."

" I'm sure I don't know what will become of us," chimed in the Public Rhymester. " I am thinking of emigrating and letting myself out on hire at people's houses in some country where Kings and Queens are not quite so plentiful as they are here. I have drawn up a little Prospectus. You might like to see it, and if you could recommend me to a good family where they know how to treat a King properly I should be much obliged," and the late Public Rhymester handed Boy the following :—

" HIS MAJESTY THE KING OF ZUM

ATTENDS PARTIES AT MOST
REASONABLE TERMS.   DISTANCE NO OBJECT.

" Oh ! kings are plentiful to-day ;
And if you want one, step this way,
My modest terms to hear.
You hire me by the day or week,
Eightpence an hour is all I seek,
My washing and my beer

" Suburban dinner parties, hops,
The Opera and ' Monday Pops '—
Why, I'm the very man.

The Missing Prince.

You really seldom have the chance
Your social status to advance
    By such an easy plan.

" Just think how Smith and Jones will stare,
And Robinson and Brown will glare,
    If to your house they come,
And you with easy, careless grace
Can introduce us face to face,
    ' My friend the King of Zum.'

" And then when nobody's about
There's heaps of little things, no doubt,
    That I could find to do.
It's seldom that you find a King
So handy about everything,
    And yet so regal too.

" When in my Royal Robes I'm drest,
I'll be most gracious to each guest,
    Attending your ' At Home.'
And when they've gone I will not scorn
To mend your children's clothes, if torn,
    Or hair to brush and comb.

" You give a Dinner—just so—look—
I'll help the Footman—Butler—Cook,
    Before the guests arrive.
In fact, I humbly claim to be,
Without the slightest question, *the*
    Most useful King alive."

"Can you suggest any improvement?" he asked when Boy had finished reading the Prospectus.

"No," replied he, "I think it reads very well indeed, and I hope that you will soon get an engagement."

"I intend going into trade," remarked the late Adver-tiser General from the throne at the other end of the room. "So many of the nobility now open shops that I don't see why Kings should not do so too. I intend to establish some Stores at Zum, and call it the 'Royal Service Supply Association for providing Kings and Queens and other members of Royal families with the necessaries of life!' You see something of the kind must be done or we shall all starve."

",Yes, I think that is a capital idea," said Boy. "I will ask King Smith I. to deal with you when I get back to the Palace; but I must be going now. Good-afternoon, Your Majesties," and Boy bowed politely, and was just going out of the door when he heard both of the Kings hurriedly scrambling down from their thrones. He waited to see what they wanted, and when they reached him, each King caught hold of one of his arms, and whispered in his ear,—

"Would you mind inviting me home to tea?"

"Oh! certainly, come by all means, if you like," said

Boy, remembering that there were lots of things left in the larder.   ·

"Thank you awfully," said the Advertiser King.

"Much obliged," echoed the other, and hurrying down the stairs and out into the street the three Kings went arm-in-arm to the Palace.

CHAPTER XI.

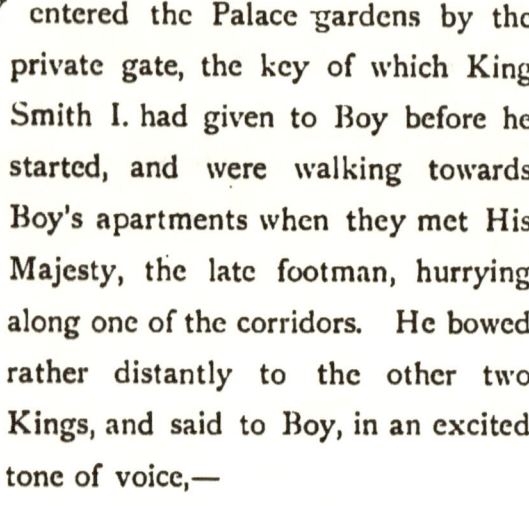

HEY entered the Palace gardens by the private gate, the key of which King Smith I. had given to Boy before he started, and were walking towards Boy's apartments when they met His Majesty, the late footman, hurrying along one of the corridors. He bowed rather distantly to the other two Kings, and said to Boy, in an excited tone of voice,—

"I've found the Portmanteau!"

"Never!" cried Boy.

"Yes," replied King Smith I., "I was sitting having my tea, when suddenly it dropped down from somewhere on to the tea-table. I can't think where it came from. Come and see it"; and he led the way to his apartments, where, sure enough, there was the Portmanteau, about which such a fuss had been made. It was quite an ordinary-looking one, but there could be no mistake as to whom it belonged, for there were the words

"*H.M. the King of Limesia.*

His Bag"

written on it, and below in smaller letters—

"*Steal not this bag for fear of shame,*
For on it is the owner's name."

"Where can it have come from?" asked Boy, gazing at it curiously.

"I can't think," replied King Smith I., "unless Ohah had something to do with it. I shouldn't be at all surprised if he had a finger in the pie."

"Perhaps," suggested Boy, "he made it invisible like the Prince and Princess, and now that he is a Kottle his charms have lost their power."

"Very likely," agreed the others. And then the question arose, "What should be done with it?"

Boy thought it ought to be sent back to the King of Limesia, but the others said "No! let him send for it, or come for it himself if he wants it;" and King Smith I.

thought that an advertisement ought to be sent to the papers, worded something like this

FOUND

A RATHER SHABBY PORTMANTEAU,

belonging to some king or another.   If not claimed within the next ten days, will be sold to defray expenses.   The finder expects to be handsomely rewarded.

They could not come to any definite arrangements about it, though, and it was placed in the corner of the room while they had their tea.

During this meal Boy was rather silent, for he was hatching in his own mind a little plot, in which the Portmanteau was to play an important part.

"How far is Limesia from here?" he asked casually, while tea was going on.

"Oh! not far," was the reply; "it is the adjoining kingdom, just through the Grim Forest, you know."

Boy knew where the Grim Forest was, for it had been pointed out to him from one of the Palace windows—a great dark-looking wood stretching away as far as the eye could see.

"Is there no other way of getting there?" he asked anxiously.

"No," was the reply, "that is the only way;" and Boy sat thinking and thinking till tea was over and the other Kings went home; then he suggested to King Smith I. that he should take charge of the Portmanteau till the King of Limesia sent for it, and this having been agreed to, he carried it up to his own apartments.

"If I can only get it to the King of Limesia," he thought, "he would no doubt be very pleased, and perhaps would advise me what I ought to do about fetching the little King back again;" for you see Boy was greatly worried at the way in which things were going on at Zum; he felt that with so many Kings and Queens about there was a great danger of the country coming to grief.

So as soon as he could he manfully set out from the Palace quite alone to try and find his way through Grim Forest to Limesia. He had discarded his paper crown and sceptre and carried the precious Portmanteau—which fortunately was not very heavy—on his shoulder. He was rather alarmed at the prospect of his journey through the dark forest, but he was a brave, sturdy little fellow, and determined to make the best of it. He commenced whistling as he entered the wood, and had not gone far when he saw an old man gathering sticks.

"Can you please tell me, is it far to Limesia?" he asked.

"Eh?" said the man, putting his hand to his ear.

"Is it far to Limesia, please?" repeated Boy.

"Ay! that's what I told her!" said the old man, shaking his head, "but she would put the onions into it. I told her the gentlefolks would be sure not to like 'em."

"You don't understand me," shouted Boy; "I want to know the way to Limesia."

"I dare say they have, I dare say they have," replied the old man; "use is no odds in these parts, sir."

"Oh dear me!" thought Boy, "he's dreadfully deaf; I shall never make him hear, I am afraid"; and he was just going to walk away when he saw an old woman in a red cloak hobbling towards them with the aid of a crooked stick.

"My husband is very deaf," she said, "and cannot hear a word you say. Can I do anything for you, sir?"

"Oh, I was only asking the way to Limesia," said Boy.

"Why, you can't go there to-night!" said the woman;

"it's ever so far; you had better stay at our cottage till the morning."

Boy thanked her very gratefully, for he really did not care for the long walk through the woods by himself.

The old woman gave her husband a poke with her stick, and pointed to the cottage which Boy could see in the distance; and the old man nodded his head, and led the way with the bundle of sticks on his shoulder, while Boy and the old lady followed behind.

"What a beautiful old house!" exclaimed Boy, when they reached the cottage; for it was indeed a lovely place, quite overgrown with climbing roses, which were just then in full bloom. There were nice old-fashioned, latticed windows with pretty white curtains and quaint twisted chimneys above the roof, and altogether it was a charming old place.

"Why, it must be a great deal too big for you and your husband, surely," said Boy, as they entered the wicket gate which led into the little garden before the cottage.

"Oh, it doesn't belong to us," explained the woman; "it was the late King of Zum's Hunting Lodge, and we live here rent free as caretakers. We have the kitchen and two small rooms, and the rest of the house has been occupied this last five years or more by gentlefolks," said

"'WHY, YOU CAN'T GO THERE TO-NIGHT!' SAID THE WOMAN."

the old woman dropping her voice to a whisper and looking up nervously at the upper windows. "But come you in and have some supper; that is, if you don't mind having it with us," and the kind old soul led the way to the kitchen, which was scrupulously clean, and Boy sat down on a little three-legged stool while she made some milk hot in a caldron over the wood fire which was alight on the old-fashioned hearth.

Presently a bell rang and the old woman asked Boy to watch that the milk didn't boil over while she went upstairs to wait on the gentlefolks.

She came down a minute or two afterwards with a piece of paper which she handed to Boy.

"Will you please tell me what is written on there?" she said. "It's getting dusk, and my poor old eyes are not so good as they used to be."

"*We shall not require anything else to-night, and please let breakfast be ready by nine o'clock to-morrow morning,*" read Boy.

"Oh! that's all right then," said the old woman, pouring out the milk into some basins for their supper.

"But why don't they tell you what they want instead of writing it?" asked Boy.

"They can't," explained the woman; "they are invisible

and speechless. It's a very sad story," she said, sighing sorrowfully.

" Why, I know a lady and gentleman who are invisible too," exclaimed Boy, thinking of the Crown Prince and the Princess. " I wonder if they can possibly be the same."

" These gentlefolks have only been like that for a few months," said the woman ; " they came here four or five years ago, a beautiful lady and a fine handsome young gentleman with one servant, a rather stout, pleasant-spoken woman, and lived here very quiet. I think the lady must have been some one very important at one time, for when their little baby boy was born quite a lot of grand folks came to see her from Limesia. Such a dear little fellow he was, and his father and mother were so proud of him and so fond of each other. The lady would sing and play beautifully, and the gentleman would read to her, and sometimes they would go out for a ride in the Forest ; but never very far away, and they always seemed glad to be back again ; till one day about two months ago a grand gentleman came and told us the King of Zum was dead, and then our gentleman, as I call him, went to Limesia with the dear lady his wife. I wish you could have seen them go. Such a lovely dress the lady had on, and beautiful jewels, and the gentleman too looked very grand.

Well, they drove off in a carriage and pair and we didn't see any more of them all day, but in the evening, though, they came back, and you never saw such a sight in all your life ; they both seemed to be fading away—bits of the gentleman here and there were quite transparent, and the dear lady had to be carried upstairs, for she couldn't walk. The next day they were much worse, and gradually disappeared altogether. Just before they vanished entirely a lot of ladies and gentlemen came over to see them from Limesia, and when they had gone back the nurse took the little boy away too, and I have never seen them again from that day to this. I suppose the lady and gentleman are still here, for every day I find on the table upstairs some written directions about meals and so on, which I carry up and which disappear too, but I never see anybody "

" Why, I do believe," exclaimed Boy, " that it must be the Prince and Princess. I *should* like to see them."

" So should I," said the woman.

" Do you think I might write them a note ?" asked Boy. " I have something very important to tell them if they are really the Prince and Princess."

" I never tried that," said the woman ; " you can do so, though, if you wish. I will take the note upstairs and put it on the table, and we will see what happens, if you like."

Boy thought that this would be the best thing for them to do, so as soon as supper was over he wrote the following polite note :

"To His Royal Highness The Crown
Prince of Zum.

"Dear Sir,

The King of Limesia's Portmanteau has been found, and a little boy from Zum has brought it here and would very much like to tell you what is happening there, because he really thinks that you ought to interfere.

"Yours respectably,
"Boy."

He meant "respectfully," of course, but you know how it is with letters. One often writes the wrong word, don't they ? I know I do. Well, this note was taken upstairs and put on the table, and presently the bell rang again violently, and on going upstairs they found another note beside it addressed to

"*Master Boy.*"

He opened it at once and found the following words :

"Ohah promised that as soon as the Portmanteau was found we should be made visible again, so please take

"AS SOON AS SUPPER WAS OVER HE WROTE."

the Portmanteau in one hand and say, ' I wish the Crown Prince of Zum and the Princess his wife to become visible again as Ohah the Magician promised.' "

Boy ran downstairs for the Portmanteau, and grasping the handle .firmly with one hand repeated the words loudly.

They were hardly out of his mouth before a thin mist appeared at one end of the room which gradually divided and became more and more distinct, till Boy could at last distinguish the outlines of the Prince and the Princess, and in a very few moments he had the pleasure of seeing them quite clearly.

"Ah! that's better," said His Royal Highness, with a sigh of relief, when he was quite solid. "How do you feel, my dear?" he asked, turning to the Princess, who, however, could not answer him yet, as only the upper part of her head had appeared at present; she waved her hand, though, to show that she was all right.

"I'm sure we are very much obliged to you," said the Prince graciously to Boy. "How did you know we were here?"

And then Boy had to tell them all about his visit to Zum and the extraordinary events which had been happening since he had been there.

"And you are quite sure that my son is all right?" inquired the Prince anxiously.

Boy explained how he had sent him to Drinkon

College under the charge of the Nurse and One-and-
Nine.

And the Princess, who had by this time quite recovered
her voice, thanked him over and over again for all that he

"GRASPING THE HANDLE FIRMLY WITH ONE HAND
HE REPEATED THE WORDS."

had done, and after arranging that the Portmanteau should
be sent to the King of Limesia the next day they
determined that it would be best for them to go back to
Zum that very night.

So the Prince's horse was saddled, and with the Princess on a pillion behind and Boy on a pony which belonged

to the little King they rode back through the gathering darkness to Zum.

All was quiet when they reached the Palace, and Boy led the way through the private entrance. King Smith had not yet retired to rest and came forward when he heard them enter. He recognised the Crown Prince at once, and hastily tearing off his own crown and cloak, bowed low and welcomed him back to the Palace.

"It is indeed a good thing for Zum, Your Highness, that you have returned," he said, "for things could not possibly have gone on like this much longer. I am sure there is not a King in the place who will not feel it a pleasure to abdicate in favour of Your Highness."

"Thanks!" remarked the Prince. "Now can we go to my own suite of rooms, or have they been altered during my long absence?"

"They are just as Your Highness left them," answered the footman, leading the way to another part of the Palace, and the Prince with the Princess leaning on his arm followed, after they had both shaken hands heartily with Boy and wished him good-night.

CHAPTER XII.

THE CONCLUSION OF THE WHOLE MATTER.

 F course the news of the Crown Prince's return was soon known throughout the kingdom, and all the Kings and Queens being thoroughly tired of the complications which had arisen through there being so many of them elected, were quite delighted to hear of it.

"For what is the use," Boy heard one of them say, "of reigning if you have no subjects to rule over but a lot of stuck-up Kings and Queens who think too much of themselves to treat other people with proper respect? I'm heartily sick of it."

"Yes," was the rejoinder, "and so am I. Why, ever

since my wife has been a Queen she has been as disagreeable as she can possibly be, and insists upon 'standing on her diginity,' as she describes it, at home. I mustn't call her 'my dear' if you please, it's too familiar—'Your Majesty' this, and 'Your Majesty' that, is what she likes, till I'm tired of hearing it. I shall be right glad when she is plain Jane Eliza Scroggs again, that I shall."

Quite early on the morning after the Crown Prince's return Cæsar Augustus Maximilian Claudius Smith (once more called Thomas for short) was sent to Drinkon College to bring the Royal Nurse and the little King home again, and while he was gone the Prince and Princess drove out in a beautiful carriage and pair and were received with most enthusiastic cheers and applause by the populace; and in the afternoon the little King returned accompanied by Mrs. Martha Matilda Nimpky.

Boy was quite surprised to see that her corkscrew curls were now a bright golden colour, whereas they had been quite black before.

One-and-Nine did not come back with them, but the Royal Nurse had a letter from him addressed to Boy, which he took up to his room and read.

"EXPENSIVE SIR," it began.

" I wonder whatever he means ? " thought boy. " Oh ! I see, ' expensive ' is his way of writing ' dear.' "

"EXPENSIVE SIR,

This comes hopping that you are most healthful, as it leaves me at present. You will be joyed to hear that I am about to be matrimonialized to a Zuluish lady of the richest colour—with movable joints. That Majestuous lady the Royal Nurse having declined me with much pleasure, has offered to be sisterish to me; but the Zuluish lady objects, so I have had to separationize myself from the Majestuous one with considerable distance. Before we parted I begged for one of those most twistful corkscrew curls as a keepsake, and she extravaganteously presentuated me with the lot—they fasten behind the head with considerable stringiness, or it may be even black tapeishness; it is hard to tell which is what in this life.

" *The Prince of Whales has given me a new coat—of paint—and as my Zuluish lady dresses with much simpleness, we shall doubtfully domesticate with great happiness.*

" *Please give my devotionated affection to that Majestuous lady, and say I will think of her with much continuation and perpetuatiou, and also the curls, which shall never leave my head—as it leaves her at present.*

" *Yours contentuously,*

" ONE-AND-NINE

" *N.B.—She had another set in her box.*"

" I suppose he means another set of curls," thought Boy, "which would account for the change in Mrs. Martha Matilda Nimpky's appearance. Well, I'm sure I hope that One-and-Nine will be happy with his Zulu bride. What a funny chap he is, to be sure ! "

Later on in the day the Prince and Princess and the little King held a reception, to which all the principal inhabitants of Zum were invited, and, of course, all the Court dignitaries were present. The Public Rhymester was also there, through the influence of his friend the Advertiser General.

The Prince made a speech from the Terrace, in which he informed the people that he should, of course, take the reins of office himself now, and would do his best, when King of the Country, to promote the welfare of his subjects.

The Princess was most popular too, and by her beauty and condescension captivated all hearts.

In the evening there was an *al fresco* concert in the beautiful Palace gardens, which were brilliantly illuminated for the occasion. Amongst the items on the programme were some songs by the " Pierrot Troupe," and Boy anxiously wondered if *his* Pierrot would be amongst them. To his great delight he found that he was, and when he stepped forward with his banjo, and began the well-known tune to "The Little Tin Soldier," Boy ap-

"'WE SHALL DOUBTFULLY DOMESTICATE WITH GREAT HAPPINESS.'"

plauded vigorously. The words, however, were quite different, and went somehow like this—

THE MARRIED TIN SOLDIER.

One night as I paused by the Nursery door,
    And looked at the scattered toys,
I said to myself, "Was there ever before
    Such troublesome girls and boys?"

And then as I hurried to gather them up,
  I heard a wee voice complain,
"Oh! sorry am I that I ever was wed,
  And would I were single again!"

On the ground at my feet lay a soldier red,
  And I think he was made of tin,
And I noticed the paint on the top of his head
  Was getting remarkably thin.
And I asked him why, at that hour of the night,
  He was making that horrible noise;
And I told him to stop and behave like a man,
  Or like other respectable toys.

"Oh! how would you like it yourself," quoth he,
  "To be married to such a wife;
To be treated as no loving husband should be,
  And be plagued almost out of your life?
She carries on with the other toys,
  She's extravagant and vain;
No wonder," he said, "that I'm sorry I wed
  And long to be single again."

"It's all very well," said another voice,
  "But he's just as bad as me,
And he needn't have wed, for I had my choice
  Of *many* as good as he."
And a waxen doll, in a dress of blue
  That was rather the worse for wear,
Looked up from under our Baby's shoe
  With a discontented air.

"You naughty, naughty toys," I cried,
"To quarrel now you're wed."
And as I packed them side by side
I sadly shook my head.
To think that this man and his wife
To such extremes should go—
How glad I am that in this life
We never quarrel so!

"Dear me!" thought Boy, "I suppose that is the same Dolly-girl and Tin Soldier that he sang about before. Well, One-and-Nine has the best of the bargain after all, if it is true; I must ask Pierrot about it if I get a chance of speaking to him."

While the concert was still going on a Messenger arrived from the King of Limesia saying that he was very pleased to have his Portmanteau again, and that he had quite forgiven his daughter for marrying the Prince now, and wished them every joy and happiness; and sent them as a peace-offering a number of Flying Machines, which had just been invented by one of his subjects, and which were most popular at Limesia.

"Flying is now the popular craze of the day in our land," explained the Messenger, "and the Park is reserved certain hours in the day for the convenience of 'Flyists.' Ladies now hold their 'At Homes' at the top of the highest trees, and Flying Tours are all the rage."

The machines, of which forty or fifty were sent, were very simple, and consisted of two large silk and whalebone wings, fastened on to the back with straps. Another strap was fastened at the wrist, and by flapping one's arms about it was possible to fly quite comfortably.

His Absolute Nothingness the Public Rhymester had to try one first.

"For," as the Lord High Adjudicator explained, "if he is killed it doesn't matter in the least."

He got on very well, though, and then some of the others ventured to try them, and amused themselves and the rest of the Company by flying up into the trees and down again. Boy tried a pair, but thought them very clumsy. I suppose that really they were too big for him.

"Not so comfortable as sailing in the Moon, is it?" said a voice by his side, and looking around Boy beheld Pierrot with his banjo under his arm.

"Oh, how do you do?" cried Boy, holding out his hand. "I'm so glad to meet you again."

"How have you been enjoying yourself?" asked Pierrot.

"Oh! immensely, thanks," replied Boy; "but I was beginning to wonder how I should get home again.

"BOY TRIED A PAIR, BUT THOUGHT THEM VERY CLUMSY."

Of course you can take me back in the Moon, can't you?"

"Oh yes, if you like," said Pierrot, "but we are starting soon and if you are coming with us you had better make your adieu to the Prince and Princess at once."

Boy arranged to meet Pierrot in a few moments by the Bandstand and then hurried off to say good-bye to his friends.

"Oh! must you go?" cried the Prince. "I'm so sorry. I wanted to ask you such a lot of questions about the government of the country that you come from, with a view to adopting somewhat the same system here; but, of course, if you must go you must. Can't you tell me just a little bit about it before you go, though?"

"Well, Your Highness," said Boy, "I really don't know much about Politics, but you see we have a lot of gentlemen in England who are called Members of Parliament who are elected from all parts of the country, and they sit every day and talk about the affairs of the nation. They have such a lot to talk about that *sometimes* they have to sit there all night, and bring sandwiches and things in their pockets to eat, or they would starve. Ladies are invited to these meetings, and sit up in the gallery to prevent the Liberals from

13

quarrelling with the Conservatives, because of course it would be very rude to quarrel before ladies, wouldn't it?"

"But what are Liberals and Conservatives, and what do they want to quarrel for?" asked the Prince.

"Oh! I don't know exactly," said Boy; "but they take sides in Parliament, you know, and one side wants to keep everything the same as it has been for hundreds of years, and the other side wants to alter everything— and they are always squabbling about this."

"But why doesn't the King stop it?" asked the Prince.

"Oh! our Kings and Queens never meddle with Politics; they only sign things, and confer titles, and hold Drawing Rooms, and open Hospitals, and Convalescent Homes, and Orphanages, and that sort of thing. They let the Members of Parliament settle all the other matters themselves. I'm afraid I haven't made it very clear, but I must be off now, Your Highness," and after shaking hands with the Prince and Princess, Boy hurried back to the Bandstand, where he found Pierrot and the rest of the Troupe waiting for him in the Moon.

· The Prince's guests were all curiously crowding around

them, and as they started they gave a hearty cheer while the Moon rose slowly up into the air and the Pierrot Troupe struck up a lively tune on their banjoes.

Before they had gone very far, however, Boy could

" ' YOU CAN'T POSSIBLY ALL GET IN,' CRIED BOY."

see that the Busybody Extraordinary and several of the other guests were hastily fastening on their wings.

"Surely they are not going to try to fly up here!" he cried.

They were, though, and in a very few moments he could see that about forty or fifty of the guests were flying rapidly towards them.

"Good gracious!" cried Boy, "they can never all get in here; we shall be upset. Go back!" he shouted, leaning over the Moon, "go back!"

But nearer and nearer they flew, till presently the Lord High Adjudicator's head appeared at .the side of the Moon, then the Advertiser General, and immediately afterwards six or seven others were scrambling over the side.

"Pray be careful. You can't possibly all get in," cried Boy; "we shall certainly be overbalanced;" but no one heeded him, and more and more people came tumbling in till, just as Boy had feared, the ;Moon lurched to one side, and then when they all rushed to the other, turned completely upside down, and out they all tumbled. Boy screamed and shut his eyes in his fright as he felt himself falling down and down and down, till crash—bang!—crash! and Boy found himself struggling on his back; he opened his eyes, and—would you believe it?—he was in his little strange bed at Scarboro', the sun was streaming through the window and the servant was knocking at the door and saying, "Your shaving water, sir," for he had mistaken Boy's room for his Uncle's.

"Well, I can't believe it has all been a dream," he

thought as he got up and dressed himself. "I shall certainly ask Pierrot about it when I see him on the sands."

But when later on in the morning he did see Pierrot, that amusing gentleman declared he had never been to Zum in his life, and asked Boy *where it was*, which was such a puzzling question that Boy has never been able to answer it to this day.

THE END.

Printed by Hazell, Watson, & Viney, Ld., London and Aylesbury

www.ingramcontent.com/pod-product-compliance
Lightning Source LLC
Chambersburg PA
CBHW020616030726
47497CB00007B/2273